THE IMMINENT SCOURGE

J.D. ANDERSON

SEVERED PRESS
HOBART

THE IMMINENT SCOURGE

WWW.SEVEREDPRESS.COM

ISBN: 978-1-925597-00-4

CONSEQUENCE

It was morning in the city. Geometric buildings stood tall against an even, empty sky. The golden sun was hidden behind them, but they caught its light, reflected it among their glass faces, and then cast it down to the streets below as though it were their own.

Paul Stott walked down the sidewalk, pale and surreal shadows cast all about him, radiating out from his feet. Even though he was surrounded by people, he felt isolated, like a single player on a stage. Something about the light gave him a feeling of centrality and of centeredness—everything in its right place, including him.

Although it was early, the air was warm. The day would be hot. Already the sidewalk had begun to stink. It was with some relief that Paul ducked into the coffee shop. The shop was more humid than the open air, but it smelled invitingly of espresso and steam.

Waiting for Paul at a sunlit table made of golden wood was Cornelius Randolph. When Paul entered the shop, Cornelius rose and went to the door to meet him. Cornelius worked his way through the growing queue of customers waiting for coffee who, in order to fit into the shop, had formed a blob rather than a line. At last, he met Paul at the entrance and shook his hand. Paul returned the gesture, saying that he hoped Cornelius had not been waiting long, to which Cornelius replied that of course he had not.

Paul was in his thirties, tall, with dark hair and an angular face. He dressed down and carried himself almost defensively, with his hands in his pockets and his head bent down a little and thrust

1

forward; had his reputation not preceded him, he would have suggested to Cornelius a poor graduate student or a garden-variety beatnik coffee-shop frequenter. Cornelius was an older man, well-dressed and with a head of full white hair. He looked somewhat out of place. Paul thanked Cornelius and excused himself to get a coffee, waiting in line for a good fifteen minutes before returning with a simple cappuccino.

Cornelius had waited for Paul before drinking the last of his espresso, and by now it was cold and bitter, and sludgy with sediment. Paul took a sip of his cappuccino and then leaned forward earnestly.

"I know that you are a busy man, and I don't want to waste any of your time," Paul said.

"I've read your proposal," Cornelius returned, setting his empty cup on its saucer. "Honestly, I'm on the fence. It seems to me that the money could be put to better use elsewhere, for more urgent needs."

Paul nodded, composing himself and letting Cornelius finish.

"You're a reasonable man, Dr. Stott?" Cornelius said. "You know all about what's going on the other side of the world, don't you?"

"Sure, I know."

"And of all of the domestic issues that we're dealing with?"

"Of course."

"Well then, I will put the question to you bluntly. Why is it that your, ah, anti-aging research is worthy of time and money, considering all of the other issues going on in the world that also require time and money, that seem more prudent, if not more of a moral imperative? You see, if a family is starving in the Middle East, why should I indulge myself in a longer life?"

Paul nodded. Then he leaned forward like a chess player who had been feigning dispassion over a game that was well in his hand.

"Well, you know, I've had this conversation before. I ask people, first of all, *what* is wrong with those wars over there, those people starving, those people dying? Why does it *matter?* And the answer is, well, it's suffering, and it's death. We don't want people to suffer and die. Now, what is the one thing that we can be sure will happen to us, but the one thing that we spend our entire lives trying to avoid? The thing that drives people to despair, some into panic, or even phobia? Death. And second to that, the only other certainty we have in this life is that we will suffer—the only choice seems to be how, or when. Now, unless death happens to you early, what is the *number one* cause of suffering in the world, the type of suffering that you are *guaranteed* to have? Aging. The effects of aging. We don't call them that—we call them by their specific names: osteoporosis, cardiovascular disease, Alzheimer's disease, cancer. But all of these, if you were to classify them, are the result of aging—they are only some malfunction or unfortunate byproduct of metabolism, cellular reproduction, and the like. And these, when they're grouped all together—the diseases caused by or more common during aging—are by far the single greatest cause of death in the world. More than war, more than starvation."

"So you want to *stop* aging, so that you can *stop* dying?"

"Well, essentially, although that's somewhat a mischaracterization of the research. Aging is the natural result of the metabolic process that is a natural part of all of us humans. That process is extremely complex, and tinkering with it, especially with our limited knowledge, could be very dangerous. So rather than trying to *change* how metabolism *works*, we are merely working to mitigate it—to either minimize or eradicate all of the *effects* of it—and therefore eradicate the *symptoms* of aging, not aging itself. Let me use an example. You know that your standard automobile has an internal combustion engine. Combustion is a chemical reaction that produces a lot of energy, but there is also some waste, usually in the form of exhaust, smoke, things like that. Now, if you want your car to keep running as long as possible, what do you do? What you *don't* do is try to change how the combustion reaction itself *works*—that's probably an impossible task no matter who you are. But what you *do* is you get the oil changed, you get the engine serviced—if something breaks you get it replaced—"

"And that's what you want to do with the human body," Cornelius said.

"Yes, exactly."

Cornelius leaned back, pressing together his lips in an expression like discomfort. He looked long and hard at the table, even though there was nothing on it except for his empty cup.

"Sounds like a long shot," he said at last. "Still sounds to me like my money would be better spent in humanitarian aid, helping people who are actually, really and truly suffering, rather than on a gamble that maybe one day—"

"Are you saying that the aged and infirm are not really and truly suffering?" Paul leaned farther forward, resting his elbows on the table, cupping his hands together and placing them under his chin.

Cornelius crossed his arms. "I don't doubt that they are. But they've lived their lives. At least, I hope they have. And if they haven't, and they've reached that age, well then, it's their—"

"So, because they're old, their lives are less valuable?"

Cornelius knit his brow and frowned into his empty cup. "Well, now—"

"And are you going by numbers? Because if you are, you're beat there too. So you send some money in humanitarian aid overseas, and you save a handful of lives. Meanwhile, how many people have died *that day* from diseases of old age, diseases that we may be on the cusp of making preventable and obsolete? And sending money overseas doesn't *actually* solve the conflict over there itself. You haven't uprooted radical Islam or Jihadism. So what then? The conflict continues, more lives are in jeopardy, and now—you're out of money."

Cornelius looked up at him with cold, alert eyes.

"You see my point, right?"

Cornelius nodded, still frowning. At length, he said, "But what good is your research if people are being killed off by violent extremism? Even if you are *able* to cure or—mitigate—the diseases of aging, won't it be irrelevant in the long run as long as we are prey to these people?"

"Well, violence will always pose a threat. Even accidents will continue to occur. But I'm saying that right now our survival rate is zero. If you can raise that statistic, even a little bit, it will be the greatest service you could possibly perform for humanity."

"Meanwhile, you just let people on the other side of the world die?"

"Nonsense, I didn't say that. The benefits of this research will extend all around the world as soon as it's been researched and developed enough to be affordable to do so. Posterity will be a moot concern—childbearing will be a matter of complete choice, not a necessity for survival. Think of all of the money that will be saved in childbirth costs, childcare, education…"

Cornelius smiled at this and unfolded his arms. "All right," he said. "I've heard enough of this malarkey."

But Paul continued to lean forward. "So now it's malarkey? Scientific research is malarkey? Ending suffering and death, that's malarkey?"

"Your whole point of view is just nonsense, it's simply backwards. I'm all for scientific progress as much as the next man, but—"

"Well, scientific progress only happens as long as there's money behind it. And unless we figure out a solution for the long-term problems of aging and death—two problems that we've faced for the entire history of the human race that we're just now on the verge of being able to beat—we're just going to keep saving people from international conflict for—for what? For a life of pain and disease? A life of, essentially, slow and painful death?"

Cornelius sighed and stood from the table. "Well, thank you, at least, for the *interesting* point of view. I wish you luck in finding your funding elsewhere, Dr.—"

Paul had not moved. He still sat leaning forward at the table, his hands under his chin. "So you just want to die? If I pulled out a gun right now… you, and your kids, and your kids' kids… because you're all dead anyway. You're all dead."

Cornelius said no more and turned abruptly from the table, taking his cup with him. He made his way through the cluster of customers, placed the cup carefully in the bus bin, and walked out of the coffee shop.

Paul had not even taken a drink of his cappuccino yet beyond the first sip. He looked down at the cup, still nearly full, with an indentation in the foam where he had sipped it. He wanted to finish his coffee, but now he had nothing to do and he figured he should get back to the lab. He had gotten a porcelain cup, expecting to have spent more time with Mr. Cornelius Randolph, so he could not take it with him. But there was nothing worse than chugging coffee, so it seemed that he was committed to spending time at the coffee shop doing nothing but drinking his coffee, whether he liked it or not. He was stuck.

A customer lightly touched Paul on the shoulder and indicated the empty space where Cornelius had been. "May I sit here?"

"Sure, man," Paul said, lifting his cappuccino to take another sip.

The man who sat across from Paul took a laptop from a bag, along with a stack of books, a notebook, and a pencil. Before long, he had filled almost the entire table with his belongings.

Can't he find another place to work on his graduate thesis, or whatever the hell it is that he's doing? Paul wondered.

With a pang of angry regret, Paul poured the rest of the cappuccino down his throat in a single draft. Then he rose, gripping the cup with his fingers clamped tightly around the rim, and dropped it in the tub. Then he exited the shop.

***

His place of work was not far, and he was able to make the walk in under twenty minutes. Although as a researcher, writer, and speaker he was affiliated with the Foundation for Aging Research and Treatment, he was currently overseeing a team working out of the facilities at the Institute for Biological Science, which itself was part of a larger conglomerate and housed on several floors of a large, mostly medical research facility building downtown.

When he arrived, instead of going straight to the lab, he stopped by the lab of another researcher, Eric Left, whom he had known during grad school. Eric worked in cryogenics, specializing in post-cryo revival. Eric and Paul would joke that their research, although funded by the same organization, was directed at opposite ends. Eric's research dealt with the preservation and revival of bodies, and so depended on the imminence of death as at least a motivating factor, if not as a prerequisite for revival, whereas Paul's research sought to eradicate death and thus make the need for any sort of preservation or subsequent revival obsolete. This was putting it rather simply, however, for their research did have an intersection: many people had already had their bodies frozen using Eric's techniques to be revived at a time when they could take advantage of Paul's anti-aging, and thus anti-death, research. In fact, they themselves had exchanged research— some of Eric's work in cryogenic preparation had assisted Paul in developing some techniques for longer-term cell preservation, and some of Paul's research into the natural decay of the human system had helped to inform Eric's preparatory work. Moreover, Eric argued that he and Paul were, in fact, working toward the same goal: to extend human life and minimize suffering. In cryogenics, Eric said, people stay alive for a longer period of time, and since they are unconscious, they are not suffering. In response, Paul had said that cryogenics was not "life," but would be better characterized as a type of death, but different from conventional human death because it was controlled, temporary, and reversible. Then they had agreed that they were at least both in the business of making death relative.

Eric had just made news by successfully freezing and then reviving a rabbit brain that had been preserved using a chemical technique to protect cellular and neurological structure. The rabbit was dead, but preserving live tissue for later reanimation was the next step. He was making significant progress in his research towards achieving this goal, and his assistants said that his drive was so strong that he barely slept or ate.

Meanwhile, Paul himself had hit a stalemate on a number of issues, the latest involving a specific type of age-related brain decay. There was as yet no way to replace brain cells, but there were methods for slowing the process of decay to keep the brain in a fully functional state for a longer period of time. However, just when it seemed that he had had the problem solved, decay would begin in a slightly different form, or through a different process. Furthermore, he was working with the brains of rabbits and mice; there was the potential that the human brain was not analogous. What might stop brain decay in a rat might not in a human.

As he swung by the door of the lab where Eric was working, Eric looked up from his work and gave him a wave.

"Hey, how did it go?" he asked.

"Shitty."

Eric frowned sympathetically and said, "Well, you win some, you lose some."

"So many people still take death for granted," Paul said.

"Well, that's what keeps me in business," Eric said, smiling. "I'll be able to bring them back sooner or later—but they'll need you to keep them back."

"Yeah."

Eric turned down and jotted something in a notebook.

"You want to get drinks later?" he said.

"No, thanks," Paul said. "I'm meeting up with somebody."

"All right," Eric said.

Paul left and went to his own lab, where his assistants were already busy preparing the next round of chemical trials for their investigation into brain cell loss. They worked in a large area with equipment mounted and stored around the periphery of the room, and a large open space with tables and a series of desks on which stood a bank of computers. Across this space, opposite the door, was an enclosed office where he worked as their supervisor. It was separated by a wall set with windows.

After he had entered the main area of the lab, he checked in with each of them to see if there was anything they needed. The responses were unanimous in that the only thing they lacked was manpower. They had all of the equipment and materials they needed, but progress was slow because there were not many of them. Paul was aware of this and expressed sympathy, assuring them that he was working to rectify the problem. Then he went to his office where he was busy preparing an informational and fundraising talk that he was scheduled to give at a university in Texas the following week.

He had not yet grown weary of the fundraising work. In fact, he preferred it to the lab work he had done when starting out in the field. But he *was* getting weary of rejection. He was getting weary of meeting so many people who should believe in what he was doing, and who agreed with him fundamentally, but simply wouldn't buy into his work. He was tired of winning arguments, only to have his opponents let them get carried away by their feelings. Everyone felt that there was something "wrong" about what he was doing. But what *was* it? No one could, or would, say. Some thought that it was hopeless, and when he told them as an experienced researcher and writer that it *wasn't* hopeless, they all saw fit to dismiss his more astute evaluation in favor of their own impoverished judgment. It frustrated him to no end, especially because he could not think of any other approach to take that might make the issue less volatile.

He did not judge it a failure that he could not work around it. It was not his fault that people made decisions preemptively, or emotionally rather than rationally. But he wished that he knew some way to get them to *stop*.

He worked on this speech for the remainder of the afternoon. His experience with Mr. Cornelius Randolph had taken a toll on his enthusiasm for the speech, so he made little progress. In dull resentment, and defeated by his inability to think and write, he left the office in the late afternoon, the sun low in the sky, the reflective buildings casting bronze light like a spell over the city.

***

Darcy was waiting for him at The Chapel, part of what once was a funeral home that had been converted into a bar. Some of the old pews still existed and lined the walls of the balcony as seating for booths, and a statue of Mary still stood recessed on one side between two of the orange-tinted glass windows.

Darcy was the same age as Paul—she was not young. But she was one of those rare women whose appearance benefits from age rather than suffers for it. Youth carries with it an anonymous beauty all its own, and so all young girls are pretty. But some young girls are pretty only by virtue of youth itself; it smooths over idiosyncrasies in strokes of broad and universal appeal. Age draws out the essence of a woman's features, which are more readily perceived when the attributes common to youth are removed. Darcy's appearance not only possessed an appeal independent of her youth, but age served to enhance and accentuate her appeal. Without youth's encumbrances and anonymity, she became more distinct, more unique, and more beautiful, and even the gentle creases that settled into her skin marked in welcome permanence on her face the expressions of quiet dignity, humor, assurance, and calm contentment that often crossed it as she grew gracefully into womanhood.

Darcy and Paul had been familiar for a couple of months, and the Chapel had become their usual meeting place. Things usually ended up at one or the other's apartment, and this was usually Darcy's since Paul's apartment was decidedly a bachelor pad and not as comfortable or welcoming as hers.

Paul walked into The Chapel already feeling uncomfortable, but he tried to put his feelings away. He saw Darcy and went to the table where she was sitting.

"Hi," he said. "How are you?"

"Good," she said. "How about you?"

He sighed through his nose. "I don't really want to talk about it."

She recoiled a little at his brusqueness, but smiled and said, "Okay."

A waitress came to their table and they ordered drinks—she a Manhattan, he a Hefeweizen.

After the waitress left, there was a moment's silence between them. Darcy tapped on the table with her fingers.

"Well, if you *do* want to talk about it, it's okay," she said, smirking a little at him.

"I don't."

"Well, all right, but we should probably find something else to talk about. Unless you want to just sit there and be silent about it the whole time."

He shook his head. "Well, how was your day? What did you do?"

"Well," she said, "thanks for asking. I worked. Not very exciting. We have people come in just to read the books. They never buy any of them—they never buy anything—they just come in to read. Some of these people who come in to read are pretty… 'special.' I'm not sure what to do about them. I asked Laura, my co-manager, about it, and she left it up to me. I don't know. It's probably bad for business, and it's not really what our shop is for, but I feel bad for them, you know? They're like kids, some of them. Big, smelly kids, but still just kids. They don't steal anything. But they smell bad, and I'm sure the books get a little wear from the use… I don't know. It's not like we get many customers nowadays. Printed books are so old-fashioned now. And I know that lots of the people who *do* buy the books will never read them—they're just gifts for somebody, or they're to look nice on their coffee table. Pretty ironic. The people who buy the books never read them, and the people who read the books never buy them."

Their drinks arrived. Darcy lifted the glass and put it to her lips. Even sipping the glass, her mouth turned up a little at the corners like she was still smiling.

Paul had been waiting for the head on his beer to recede. Now that it had, he took a drink, and then said, "*Language* is going to be old-fashioned soon."

She laughed a little and said, "What?"

"I'm serious," he said, looking deep into his glass. "What do we use words for? Communication, right? Communication of ideas? There's research being done right now to codify those ideas digitally. I just read an article where some scientists created an image from a man's dream—they placed terminals on his head and generated an image based on the brainwaves he was producing while he was asleep. So not much longer now and you will be able to visualize something and have it show up on a screen—or, instead of a screen, if the other end of the terminals were connected to another person's brain, then you could literally 'show' the other person what you were thinking without having to describe it using words. Words are just an intermediary. It may become possible to codify abstract ideas digitally like this and then record them, so instead of books, people may be able to connect their brains to diodes and instantaneously experience the transfer of a complex idea without the originator having to formulate it in words, or the recipient to decodify it and reconstruct it through language. Books will become even more obsolete than they already are, maybe even language itself. I mean, what if we were eventually able to do all of this *wirelessly?*"

"Shit, man, that's way over my head," Darcy said, smiling again. "What if something pops into my head that I don't want anyone to see? Yikes. I think words are a useful intermediary because it gives you a second to think before whatever it is just comes out. Besides, I have to write to think."

"You what?"

"No, I'm serious. It helps me to sit down and write. I make lists." She added ominously, "Lots of lists," smirked, and then continued, "If I'm feeling a certain way or something weird has just happened to me, I sit down and write and process what I'm going through. I mean, I guess maybe I 'know' everything in my head already, but it's almost like I don't. It's like until I write it out I'm just confused. But when I write it all out, I figure it out."

"You're weird," he said.

"*You're* weird," she returned, "talking about hooking up people's brains to *diodes* so that we don't have to have conversations. If that were true, you would never have the chance hear my *beautiful* voice. Besides, I don't think that would catch on. People like words. Shakespeare, you know?"

"I hate Shakespeare."

"Yeah, I bet you do, but lots of people just get a kick out of saying shit like, 'What a piece of work is man! How noble in reason, how infinite in faculty!' People pay money to just *listen* to that. They're absolutely tickled by it."

"I never understood any of that."

"Well, yeah. It was that stuff that got me into acting. Hamlet, especially. I always wanted to be Hamlet. Even though I'm a girl. I always thought, hey, men played women in Shakespeare's day, maybe I could be in an all-woman Shakespeare troupe. Or maybe just play Hamlet, and not even make it a thing, really. The best fucking Hamlet ever, man or woman."

"You gotta follow your dream, I guess," Paul said, taking a drink.

"I guess so," she said. She drained the last of her Manhattan just as the waitress was making a pass by their table.

"Do you want another?" the waitress asked.

"Yes," Darcy said emphatically.

Paul took another sip. He was not halfway through his.

The waitress gone, Darcy said, "So what's your dream anyway? Are you living the dream, what you do, or is there something 'out there' that you still think about?"

Paul spun his glass on the table. The coaster was stuck to the bottom with moisture and clung to the bottom of the glass, spinning with it.

"I am doing what I'm passionate about, I guess."

"You're passionate about ending aging."

"I'm passionate about life. Minimizing suffering, extending lifespan… that's what I see as… most connected to what I'm all about." He continued twirling his glass. He wondered vaguely if he could spin the glass fast enough that the coaster would break free.

"But, I mean, is the work fun for you? Doing research or… or giving talks?"

"Look, I said I didn't want to talk about it," he said, still spinning his glass. A little bit of his drink spilled out of it. He stopped the glass abruptly and lifted it and took a drink, the coaster still stuck to the bottom.

"Talk about what?"

"Talk about work. It was, well, kind of a rough day I guess, and I want to have fun, not talk about a rough day at work." He set the glass firmly back down.

"Well, okay," she said.

He started spinning the glass again, slowly. "I mean, don't you agree that life is valuable? Who doesn't agree with that?"

"Well, certainly, of course human life is valuable."

"Exactly. And the greatest good then is to make that life as good as possible for as long as possible. Maximum goodness."

"Sure."

"I mean, don't you agree?"

"Well, sure, but I don't know if I'd want to live *forever*." She was looking off to the side, studying the peaked orange glass windows. "It just seems like it would get old. I don't really want to be *around* forever. I don't know who would *want* me around forever. I guess I don't really know of anybody else, either, who would especially benefit the human race that much."

"You're saying no one *deserves* to live forever."

"Maybe. What *do* people deserve?"

"I think people are basically good. People have a right to happiness."

"Sure, but people are also fucked up." Her eyes roamed around the room. "I don't know. It just seems to me like we have so many problems, living forever won't really solve anything."

"What do you mean? Why not? Do you mean you would rather die?"

She turned back to the table, looking down at it. "Well, I mean, if your goal is the elimination of suffering... I don't know."

"What do you mean?"

"I mean, I don't know! Wouldn't it all get old after a while?"

"Well, then, that would just mean you're not doing it right."

She straightened up and broadened her shoulders, and a smile played on her face again. "I mean, what if somebody could, you know, never make it work romantically, even if they lived a very long time, and they were just tired, you know? Tired of things never working out. And that's not even the worst thing that a person can go through. In any case, isn't death the end of suffering?"

"Death *is* suffering. It's the chief form of suffering that there is!"

The smile disappeared and her face grew dark and serious, more serious than he had ever seen before.

"No," she said, "it's not. After you're *dead*, you don't feel *anything*."

Paul stopped for a moment and spun his glass at a regular tempo. "So you're okay with death?"

"What do you mean okay with death?"

"So you'd be okay dying, say, tomorrow?"

She twisted her mouth to the side and sat back. "I guess I hadn't thought about it."

"Yeah, you see, no one ever does. Not unless they're old and death is at their doorstep, as they say. But it's coming, it's coming for you, and me, and it will be here sooner than we think, and the only thing that we can do is to help ourselves—to live longer, to live better."

He was impressed with himself. He had half a mind to write it down for his talk the next week.

"Unless, of course," he added, "you'd rather be dead."

She was disinterested again. "It would be an end to suffering. Or at least an end to this fucking conversation."

"Answer me seriously. Aren't you afraid of death?"

She turned to him darkly again, her eyes flickering. "Well, I'm not afraid of *Hell.* Are you?"

"Hell?" He straightened, taken aback. "What does that have to do with anything?"

She erupted, speaking quickly in a tumble of words. "Because that's the only reason anyone would be afraid of death. Either there's *nothing*, or you go to *Heaven*, or you go to *Hell*. If it's nothing or you go to Heaven, you have nothing to worry about. So you must be afraid of Hell."

He froze, staring at her. Then he looked down and away. "You know what?" He reached into his back pocket and pulled out his wallet. "Let's try this again some other night when we're in a better mood."

Darcy looked at him incredulously.

Paul dropped a ten on the table, stood, slipped his wallet back into his pocket, and walked out. The heavy door swung shut behind him.

At that moment, the waitress returned with Darcy's second martini and said, "Sorry for the delay. There you go."

Darcy looked down into the drink, taking special note of its hue, its smell, and the way it was still rocking gently from the waitress's motion as she had set it down. Had she seen the bill on the table? Perhaps she had ignored it, not wanting to be *awkward.*

Thanks for that, thought Darcy.

Without another thought, she slugged the drink, dropped some more money on the table without really counting it, and left, plunging into the night outside the heavy door.

In an effort to clear her head, Darcy walked along in the familiar world of the city at night—streets upon streets of bars and pubs, venues and restaurants. She was unsettled, and she felt that she wanted to be away from herself, even though she knew that was not really possible. But the city and the city air and the city sights and sounds and smells had begun to distract her already, and she was thankful.

The city was life. It coursed with movement and light and sound. It seemed to never stop, and its constancy was reassuring. It repeated the same themes in a thousand different iterations of food, drink, and music. It was singularly diverse, and diverse in its singularity. It connected people to people; it was a hub of hubs. World-class food was made and tasted here, life-altering conversations were had here, historical progress initiated and enacted here—in the city.

But in the midst of this life was also death. Whatever preyed on people found its greatest promise here. The homeless wandered the sidewalks with vacant eyes, minds contracted and singularly bent toward what purposes had commandeered their lives. Others besides the homeless were dead too, looking without sight, speaking without meaning, drowning their thoughts in Lethean half-death measured out in shots, pints, and pours. They were alive, but not fully living, they were awake but not fully present. It was as though at any moment they might be awakened, and they kept themselves from it by distraction. The light, the sound, the music, the drink—all were distractions from something seen only on the edge of vision, if at all, and once glimpsed, looked away from hastily, the gaze shifted to whatever it could find next—and there was always more light, sound, music, or drink. Darcy had glimpsed it tonight, and the city was there for her—the city with all its life was there to catch her in arms of asphalt, grime, light, and color.

Just seeing it and breathing it in was enough, and Darcy walked quickly back to her apartment. The night air pouring into her lungs always seemed to remind her of her aloneness, her solitude, despite the bustle of the city, and it was a good reminder. She was alone—so she went to go be alone.

***

The next morning, Paul arrived at work early after a night of fitful sleep. He always slept poorly when something was bothering him, although this time he couldn't pinpoint what that something was. It wasn't his conversation with Darcy; he had had arguments with girls before. It wasn't his conversation with Mr. Randolph; he had been rejected before. He decided to take advantage of his restlessness and went into work early to channel his energy into working on his presentation.

After an hour or so of work, the lab technicians under his employ began to trickle in and pick up with their work. He had not made much progress, and after working for another hour or so, he gave up and went into the lab.

After working with them in the lab them for some time, his phone rang in his office. He went in, and answering the phone, he found that it was Eric.

"Hey, Paul, would you be able to talk at some point this afternoon?"

"I can talk right now."

"Okay. Well, it's something I'd rather discuss with you face to face, not over the phone. Are you available? You want me to come up there?"

"No, no, I'll come down. I'll be there in a minute."

Paul went downstairs. Eric's lab was constructed just like Paul's, with a large working area and an enclosed, windowed office adjoining it. The atmosphere in Eric's office was more upbeat than usual, and instead of working, Eric's technicians were sitting back against the tables, talking and laughing with each other. No work was being done.

Eric was with them, and upon seeing Paul, he motioned for him to follow him into his office.

"What's up?" Paul asked as Eric shut the door behind them.

"Well, we've had a pretty significant breakthrough. I don't want to bore you with the details—I know you have work to do—but

17

we've just had some of our work endorsed by the National Neuroscience Association. Also, since the rabbit brain recovery, we've actually been able to apply for a grant that we were hoping to get, and it's looking like a pretty sure thing."

Paul began, "Congratulations—"

Eric held up his hand and continued. "So, the good news is that we're getting more money. The reason I called you is that there's good news for you too: part of our next steps involves some of the work you've been doing on the brain. I will be able to siphon off some of the money we're getting for our work and send it your way, since we're going to need to piggyback on you for what we're doing next."

To Paul's own surprise, he was not happy at this news. He was not sure why, but he feigned happiness and relief, saying, "Wow! That's fantastic news. Thanks for letting me know." He faltered for a moment, and then added, "So you have the publication coming out soon?"

"Yeah, sure, you can have all the material if you want. I made copies for you."

"Okay, great."

The sinking feeling of disappointment persisted, and Paul was still not sure why he felt it. He followed Eric to the corner of his office where he had a crate full of files and accepted them when Eric handed him the box. The box was heavy, and attempting to appear as though he were not really exerting himself, Paul carried the box out of the office.

Back in his own office, Paul set the box to the side of his desk, on the floor. He reemerged to tell his team the good news. They seemed genuinely pleased at it, and this helped to lift his spirits a little. When he went back in his office and closed the door, he no longer felt as downcast as he had earlier, although he was still not as happy as he felt he should be. He sat down at his desk and put the box of files out of his mind, attempting to focus once more on his writing, which had gone terribly all morning.

He should be celebrating, he thought to himself.

He had the thought to contact Darcy, but felt hesitant after the previous evening. After a moment of deliberation, he decided to contact her, if only to shake the odd feeling that was hounding him.

***

Although he had been afraid that she wouldn't respond at all, she had, in fact, responded quickly. He arranged to meet her immediately after work, and took the bus straight to her apartment without stopping by his own.

He arrived at her apartment building as it was beginning to get dark. It was a tall old brick building near downtown. He was going to ring for her room, but another resident was on her way out, so he took the opportunity to go ahead into the building himself and go up to her apartment. It was appropriate, he thought, to surprise her. He was there to celebrate.

He climbed the two flights of stairs quickly and found her apartment, and knocked. She opened the door and smiled at him, looking surprised.

"You didn't buzz in," she said.

"Somebody else was leaving."

"Well, come in, I'm almost ready," she said.

He stepped in briskly, his hands shoved in his pockets. She turned and went around the corner toward the bedroom and the bathroom of the apartment.

"How was work?" she shouted to him from within.

"Fine," he said, looking absently around her apartment.

She emerged and placed herself in front of him, her dark eyes shining at him. She wore a long dark jacket and around her neck she wore a lightweight ornamental scarf of a deep red color that brought out the subtle flush of her lips and the richness of her eyes. She wore a white knit hat, and her dark, shining hair fell comfortably about her shoulders.

"Where did you want to go?" she asked.

He put his hands on her hips, and in turn, she placed her hands lightly on his arms. "Oh, I don't know," he said. "I had a good day at work. I wanted to celebrate."

"Oh," she said. "Well, that's good news. And I know some places that are good for celebration."

"I mean, I was thinking maybe we could hang out here for a while. You know, celebrate here for a little bit."

"Well, I'm not sure what I have. I have a ton of old vodka, probably a tablespoon of Glenlivet 12… no mixers. So unless you're down for vodka shots, we'll probably have to go somewhere else."

"No, I mean…" he said, pushing on her hips and making them sway.

She smiled up at him, and he suspected then that she had only been playing dumb.

"Let's go *some*where," she said. "I've been looking forward to going out." Her hands rested firmly on his arms. They were not restraining him, but they were prepared to.

He brought her hips closer to him, and he leaned in. She pushed back on his arms respectfully but firmly.

"Look, I can't—" she said, "I'm not going to—"

He stopped. She was looking off to the side and away, thinking about something. At last, she dropped her hands a little, down to his elbows, and held them gently.

"I was… I was really happy when you messaged me today." She pushed him away a little so that they were looking at each other face-to-face from a comfortable distance. "I felt—I felt pretty bad after last night. I felt stupid."

"Oh, don't—you're not stupid—"

"Well—I shouldn't have said what I said. I don't know… I have some baggage. I was raised in a religious family. We talked a lot about death." She looked earnestly at him for a moment, and then added, with a laugh, "And Hell."

"It's okay."

She grew serious again. "No, it's not really okay. I had no right to pester you about your beliefs like that."

"Well, okay."

"And I was really happy when you messaged me. I wasn't sure if you would want to talk to me again, you know? But even so, I didn't expect to feel as happy as I did. I mean, it was weird." She looked at him seriously, her dark eyes trying to express something to complement her words. "It was like this sense of relief, or something... it was more than just, 'happy to hear from you.'"

Paul felt another sinking feeling, but this time one that he understood, and felt that he could manage.

"You know," he said, "I don't really want things to get that serious between us..."

"I know, I know, and that's what's so frustrating. I know how you feel, and I didn't want things to get serious either. I'm not ready for it, and I don't really know, you know, if you and I could make it work long-term. But it really... it kind of spooked me!"

"I don't understand."

"Well, it's like—you and I are in this, whatever-you-want-to-call-it, casual thing. You know it, and I know it. There's nothing else that we want. But it was like there was something else in here"—she indicated her heart with her fingers—"that has always been in there, waiting, and today it got free. Like an animal got out of its cage on accident."

"I really don't understand."

"I didn't think you would, I guess," she said, drawing away a little bit in resignation. "I was just really inexplicably happy, but then afterwards, I was terribly sad. It made me sad that I had felt so happy... Just—do you ever just feel *sad*? You know, so *sad* that you can't even put it into words? And, like, when you feel it, it takes you over so much that you're not even *you* anymore, you're just this *sadness?*"

Paul scrunched up his lips. "Probably biological."

"I *know* that it's biological, but..." She threw her hands up in the air in exasperation, the attempt having utterly failed. She leaned back on the back end of the sofa. "I think back to when I was a little kid, and everything just sort of made sense. I think about how I used to not care who I *was*, I didn't really care about *being* anybody, but I was most like myself then... It's like I've lost something very important, something very special that I don't even remember. And today, the happiness I felt touched on that a little bit. I knew it was wrong, I knew that it shouldn't have touched on that, I shouldn't have let it... but it did anyway."

"All in your head."

"Well, either way, even if it's all in my head, I still have to live with it."

Paul nodded, looking at the floor.

"I'm sorry. I know it doesn't really make any sense. I have no excuse."

Paul shrugged.

"Are you all right?"

Paul shrugged again.

Darcy looked at him for a long time, and he was still looking down. "Talk to me," she said, at last.

Paul lifted his shoulders. "I don't know what to say. I guess you have the right."

She looked resigned—resigned to everything: her decision, his attitude, the unknown future, the mystery of experience.

At last, she threw her hands out to the side in surrender and something like humility. "Well, you can stay here as long as you want," she said. "But I got all dressed up, so I'm going to go out."

"You still want to go out?"

"Well—I mean, maybe it's not a good idea to go out with each *other*… But yes, I'm going out."

"All right," he said, his hands shoved deep in his pockets.

"Hey," she said. "I like you a lot." She reached out and gave his arm a squeeze. He hated the touch. "You know what they say. 'It's not you, it's me.' It is me. It's all about me. It has nothing to do with you. Okay? I want to know that you understand that."

"Okay," he said, nodding.

She smiled hopefully at him, a timid sunrise of a smile. "Okay," she said. "I'm leaving now. Just make sure to lock the door behind you."

And she left, just as she said she would.

Now, he was alone in the apartment. He looked around, the apartment empty except for him. He took a few aimless steps in, eventually making his way over to the gas fireplace insert. On the mantle over the fireplace were some decorations that he had noticed but never really examined closely. There was a matryoshka doll, separated and lined up. There a small figurine of a porcelain cat, too small for any detailed features but only two dots of paint for eyes. There was a music box, which he picked up. He turned the crank, and as it played, he heard in his head the words of the familiar tune it played:

> *Somewhere over the rainbow,*
> *Skies are blue…*

He sneered in contempt and put it back on the mantle.

From outside, he heard a commotion of voices. They were in the heart of the city, and he thought nothing of it, but he went to the window, pulled back the curtain, and looked down to the street.

A car was stopped in the middle of the road, its headlights painting a beam of yellow light down the asphalt, casting a shadow from a form that lay huddled in its beam, lying still on the ground. It was a girl, and even from that distance and in the weak light of the headlights, he could make out Darcy's deep brown hair, shining in the light like a halo around her head.

He bolted out of the apartment, throwing the door open and running down the hallway, then clambering down the stairs, swinging himself on the handle and railing. He ran out onto the street to where the body was.

Her arms were thrown out and her head tipped back, hair flaming out from it. Some of her hair was tangled about her face as though some wild animal had mauled her to death in ecstasy, the pose suggesting the motion with which she had been thrown back as though it had never ended—as though she were traveling upward, and had been frozen in time so that she would be traveling upward forever.

Paul fell to his knees next to her body, his mind racing. Examining her more closely, he saw that her hair was matted with blood and her open eyes were frozen and inert. She had the appearance of death or coma. He felt for her pulse; there was none. His throat constricted in something like revulsion.

A small crowd had gathered. The driver of the car stepped out and knelt over the body.

"Is she dead?" he asked, his voice quavering. He was an older man with light hair that was either blonde or gray—in the light, it was difficult to tell.

"No, she's alive," Paul said. Then he said, suddenly, "You need to help me take her where I can help her. I'm a doctor." When he said the words, he had a peculiar disembodied sensation, as though he were watching himself, or someone else, say them.

"Shouldn't we call an ambulance? The police?"

Paul turned on the man in electric anger, his face tight with rage. "Listen," he said, almost growling, "I'm doing you a favor. You just hit a woman crossing the street. She's going to die soon, I can tell you that. Now, if you want to wait for the cops, and face a manslaughter charge in court, you can do that—or you can help me help this woman and do us all some good!" He was tingling with adrenaline.

The man, his entire body quaking, said nothing more but held out his upturned hands in acquiescence, waiting for instructions from Paul.

"I'll support her head. You help me lift her body. We'll put her in the back. Then you take us where I tell you."

They hoisted the body, Paul lifting carefully so as not to damage the head or spine any more than they already had been. They laid the body on the faux-leather backseat bench of the car, an older, smelly Cutlass. Then they hurriedly got into the car. Outside the windows, members of the crowd looked confused, but not concerned.

"Okay," said Paul, putting on his seat belt, "just go straight. Take the right turn at 12th. Then I'll tell you what to do after that."

"Okay," said the man, throwing the car into gear.

As the car lurched forward, Paul reached out his hand behind him to brace the body in the back seat. With his other hand, he took his cell phone out of his pocket, opened it, and made a call.

"Eric," he said. "Are you in the lab? — Okay, good. I'm on my way. There's something I need from you. — Well, more of a favor, I guess. I'll be there in a few minutes; I'll explain everything to you then. — Bye."

✳✳✳

The Cutlass pulled up in front of the institute and lurched to a stop. Paul got out of the car, went to the back, opened the door, and made to pull the body out.

"Do you need my help?" the man asked, looking back nervously.

"No, I can take it from here," Paul said.

The man nodded in assent, and then looked out the window. "This ain't no hospital, is it? What is this building?"

"I'm a doctor. I do research. This is a lab. Trust me."

"Well, okay."

Paul had managed to pull Darcy's body out without too much trouble and now lay her head on his shoulder like a child's. He kicked the door shut with his foot and walked toward the building. The Cutlass sat idling for a while to Paul's great annoyance, but then it finally pulled out and gurgled away into the night.

The body grew heavy before long, and Paul barely managed to keep from dropping it as he brought it up in the elevator. As he ascended, his mind was a tangle of racing thoughts. To preserve her or to revive her was the main question. He had the technology to do both. He had been bewildered by their last conversation and was acting mostly out of a vague hope at some form of closure, or at least an understanding. He had meant exactly what he had said: that he hadn't understood. He believed that she loved him, but he struggled to understand her reasons for leaving him. He wondered what her true feelings *were*, what depth of love had really been there. He wanted to know *what* she really thought of him altogether.

And he thought that, if he were able to revive her, that now she would have a different perspective. She said she had been plagued by sorrow—was it the consciousness of death or the fear of death that caused this? And would it be different now that she had actually experienced death?

In his case, when he had seen her body, he had ceased to believe in death altogether. The change that had overcome her was a change in the state of the matter that made up her body, the cessation of certain electrical and chemical processes *called* life, and the commencement or acceleration of certain kinds of decay *called* death, all of which were correctable and reversible. She was not dead, because he had freed himself to no longer identify her symptoms as such—she was only inert. He could teach her this if she wouldn't already understand it. He could explain it to her in a way that might finally put her at rest.

He arrived in Eric's lab holding the body, her head still on his shoulder, his arm hooked under her legs, drawing them up as in a fetal position.

"I need your help," he said to Eric.

"Oh my God!" Eric exclaimed. "What the hell? Is that—is she—*dead?*"

"She was in an accident," he said. "I'm going to bring her back. You need to help me."

"What are you talking about? Is she *dead?*" Eric asked again.

"She was in an accident," Paul repeated.

"She's dead!" Eric said. "You can't bring someone back from the dead…"

Paul laid her on a table and then turned on Eric. He loomed over him. "Her brain has stopped functioning; her heart has stopped beating; she's lost some fluid—that's *all*. If you call that *death*—I call it only a *problem to be solved*. I rejuvenate her brain matter, her loss of fluid—you reanimate what's been repaired."

"It's never been done before. We've only successfully recovered the raw material, not reanimated—"

"Well, you're going to do it tonight. Start getting prepped. I'll give her the injections."

"What about the others? This could take hours, days—"

"Obviously, we don't have that long. She is deteriorating as we speak. I can only reverse the process and maintain her state for so long before she begins to decay again, and it wouldn't do well for either of us to have the others walk in on this."

"Jesus, man— take her to a hospital. I don't want any part of this."

"You want my help? My research? Or not?"

Eric drew back. "Are you threatening me?"

Paul knew that it was a pitiful threat, and he backed down.

"Look," he said. "We've been partners for a long time. If we get in trouble for this, I'll take the fall. But we won't. We'll be fine. You used to be a doctor. You know exactly what to do."

Eric was trembling.

"Don't take too long to decide," Paul said. "The longer we wait, the more difficult it will be. And the greater risk we take of someone showing up."

Eric thought deeply. "I don't know," he said. "I have a wife and kids…"

Paul scoffed. "Give me a break!" he said. "You're at work *all the time*. Even if you went to jail… what would be the difference? Your wife and kids will be *fine*."

At this, Eric looked hurt, and Paul realized that he had said more and hit harder than he had intended to. But it worked. Eric nodded, his face cast down in shame.

"Okay," he said softly. "Let's hurry up, then."

The men went to work. Paul shaved her head, cleaned the wound, stitched it and bandaged it, and then prepared a series of injections. The first was actually a large amount of saline drip to replenish her fluids. The next were based on the research he had performed—designed to repair whatever systems had been damaged at her death. Since he did not have the time or the means available to diagnose the extent of her injuries and ascertain exactly what was necessary, he went with his gut. He knew that her brain had likely suffered a great deal of damage, and had also undergone some decay. The treatment he was to administer was new, and involved the direct application of certain amino acids to the brain by injection into the subarachnoid space. Using a drill, he penetrated into her skull, creating an opening just deep enough and wide enough for the application, but without any direct contact to the brain itself. Since he was working only with the rudimentary equipment available in the lab, he could not be as precise as he would have liked. He could not be positive that he had not scored her brain with the drill. But he was working quickly and efficiently, and was fairly certain that he had not inflicted any additional damage. His other treatments involved the repair of the cardiovascular system, which he also knew was damaged due to the amount of blood loss, and the likely force with which she had been struck. These were more straightforward and took less time.

He considered what he was doing an act of love. He was restoring her to a previous, ideal state in which she would be able to apprehend him again, this time for who he really was, and understanding more clearly the things that she should understand.

Meanwhile, Eric busied himself about the lab. His task was relatively easy—if the body were properly repaired and rejuvenated, it were not much different from an emergency medical technician reviving someone from cardiac arrest. Eric called upon his powers of electrical engineering to create a makeshift defibrillator, and also prepared a round of injections based on those he had designed for cryogenic preservation, in order to stabilize what restorations Paul had made to prevent decay from beginning again before she was revived, should the process take longer than expected.

It was in the third hour of the morning that Paul finished his work and brought the body to a table that Eric had prepared. She was no longer as she had been even in the moments after her death, in the headlights of the car. Then, she had still retained some of her distinct beauty in the pose of her body and the angle of her face, adorned by the halo of hair. Now, in the lab, her face was pale, and her bald head was wrapped in bandages. The dark eyebrows and eyelashes stood out boldly against her face. She resembled an unfinished porcelain figure of a woman, imbalanced and uncanny. Paul undressed her, baring her chalk-white body to the light. Her nakedness was to him scientific and objective— neither natural nor unnatural, but simply necessary.

Eric had pulled together materials from all over the building. Paul was astounded at what Eric had managed to accomplish—it was as if Eric had performed an act of magic. It was clear that Eric was Paul's superior in ingenuity, resourcefulness… but there was no time for petty jealousy now.

Eric attached makeshift electrodes to Darcy using medical tape that he had cannibalized from a first-aid kit in the lab. He placed one just below her clavicle, and the other underneath her breast on the opposite side. From the lab next door, he had commandeered some plastic tubing and a bag. From this, he had constructed an IV, with a needle placed at the lower end of the long tube and the bag of saline suspended on a shelf near the table. She did not have any blood pressure, so it was difficult for him to find the vein, but he inserted the needle, relatively assured from his powers of intuition that he had placed it in the vein. He had also attached a separate pair of diodes that were connected to a speaker that would act as an electrocardiogram to monitor her heart once it had started to beat again.

"We need to do it now," Paul said.

Eric said, "I know." He was prepared to administer a dose of the electrical current from a machine attached by wires to the electrodes placed on Darcy's body. With the push of a button, he sent it. Her body jolted and the ECG registered sporadic beating of her heart, which it reported with a series of beeps. After the surge of electricity, the heart beat spasmodically in a flurry and then died out. Eric administered a stabilizing solution through the IV quickly by switching out the suspended bag for a syringe and then switching it back. He pressed his hands on her sternum, moving rapidly up and down. Then he went back to the machine, and he sent another shock. The heart became active again, circulating the stabilizer into her bloodstream.

Although he could not be sure, Paul felt that he observed a change come over her face—as though the coloring that she had exhibited in life had begun to return to her face and body, subtly, like fruit beginning to ripen.

Her heart beat in a more regular pattern that eventually sputtered to a stop again. Eric issued another surge of electricity— this one longer and apparently with more force. Darcy's body arched up off the table. Her fingers spread like the fingers of a bat's wing, and they were thin and yellow, appearing skeletal, convulsing with the shock. Her heart beat rapidly, but in a steady rhythm. The shock ended and the heart continued to beat. Her body collapsed limply back on the table. The ECG beeped steadily—the heart was still beating. It was rapid, and somewhat unsteady, but it was beating. She was alive.

After he had listened to the heartbeat long enough to assure him that no more shocks would be necessary, Eric collapsed backwards into a nearby chair. Paul stood over Darcy, studying all that his senses could take in. He marked that her chest was moving up and down, slowly, taking in breath. He observed that her color had returned, although under the wan light in the lab, it was difficult to truly ascertain the shade of it. Although she appeared rosy at the surface in her cheeks, her whole aspect seemed to exhibit a greenish hue underneath, of sickness or nausea. Her eyes were closed, and her lips were pale. Were it not for the movement of her chest, and the confirmation of her heartbeat by the ECG, he might still have taken her for dead. The heartbeat, which had been holding a steady beat, had gradually slowed, and still seemed to be slowing, normalizing towards a more natural tempo.

Paul was jittery with excitement, an excitement he had not felt since he was very young. It was like the excitement that he had felt as a young child on Christmas morning, when the world seemed new, all presents still unopened, his knowledge only of great joy and anticipation, and believing that the anticipation would be perfectly and completely fulfilled. It was as though he had, for the moment, reverted to some primordial state, before a knowledge of the world itself: the complications of relationships, the difficulties of adulthood, the struggle of existence.

Eric looked near death himself. He was pale and the sweat had cooled into a glistening clamminess on his face.

"You can take all of that stuff off now," he said. "I think she's done."

Paul, still leaning over the body like a vulture inspecting a carcass, seemed to awaken from some sort of trance. He peeled the defibrillating electrodes off of her body, although he left the ECG electrodes on so that he would continue to be able to monitor her heartbeat. He did not want to disturb her too much by dressing her, so he lay her clothes over her body as a covering. Her eyes were still closed, and she still looked as though she had not been completely restored to life—or, as Paul thought, what we commonly call life. This observation brought up some questions for Paul: of all the myriad activities that occur in the human body that qualify the body as "alive"—were there any that had not been reactivated? And in that case, would it matter?

He decided to wait. It was still early yet, about the fourth hour of the morning. Eric had fallen asleep in his chair. Paul was too excited to sleep, and felt as though electricity were coursing through his own body at a slow and steady current. He felt almost imbued with a power that might have been mistaken by someone else as a spiritual power, but that he knew was more like the power of knowledge, or of having witnessed a remarkable event. And a remarkable event this was in the history of science. It was unfortunate that it had been illicit—that social mores and taboos would prevent it from ever being known or celebrated.

Eventually, the excitement mellowed, although he still felt the dull tingle that anticipation leaves when its fulfillment is deferred. He took a seat beside Eric, who had slumped into a position more conducive to the onslaught of sleep that had overtaken him.

The ECG beeped, and beeped, and beeped, and as fatigue began to lightly prod at Paul with its cotton fingers, he concentrated on that sound. It had grown slow. He realized that it had been slowing ever since it had started. Its slowing down had ceased to be perceptible, but as he listened, he discerned that it was distinctly slow, too slow to really sustain any human. A shock went through him and he jumped up and resumed his former position, leaning over the body, inspecting it.

There was no perceptible change in her appearance. He watched for signs of her breathing and saw none, although he assumed that her breaths were coming very slowly now. He held his hand to her nose to see if he could feel the exhale of warm air. He felt none. The heartbeat slowed even more. He put his finger to her neck to confirm the slowness of the beat with his own touch. Her skin was not warm. It was cold and clammy. He would have taken it for lifeless *were it not so moist.*

The heartbeat became slower, and slower…

Finally, the beat stopped altogether. Shaking, Paul looked up to Eric, who was still asleep. He was about to say something to Eric, but then looked down at the body again.

The body was perfectly still except for an almost indiscernibly slow movement on the face: the eyelids were lifting. Very slowly and steadily, like the measured, automatic movement of an insect, her eyes opened. Underneath the lids, the eyes stared vacantly upward, cloudy with decay. After the eyes were open, the lids kept lifting, as though they were being pulled unnaturally by something from behind, until the whites around the irises were almost completely exposed, giving the whole face an uncanny, skull-like appearance. The cheeks were sunken and dark as with bruising or decay, and the outlines of the teeth were beginning to show against the thin, pale flesh. The lips lost their color and drew back, shrinking away from the teeth as the lids had shrunk away from the eyes. The jaws opened and took in the air with a raspy hiss, and then the head turned, the eyes shifting mechanically and finally directing themselves upon *him.*

They did not fix him in a stare, nor was it even a gaze in any sort of conventional sense. The eyes lacked life, and so any sort of look or gaze which would normally be associated with life—the look of any other creature, including a human—was absent. But the eyes were not characterized by a mere absence of this either. There was *something* else, as though lack were something concrete, manifested for the first time *in this look.* It was not the conventional form of death, which is really only characterized by a lack of life. It was a terrifying unity of nothingness and somethingness, but because of this unity, it transcended them both.

It reached out its skeletal, decomposing hand toward him, and he recoiled in abject fear, falling backward onto the equipment, knocking it away and falling to the floor in a heap.

Eric awakened at the crash. The thing turned its face toward him—the face with its awful eyes of negation and its skeletal visage in arrested decomposition—the face of neither life nor death, but of something else…

Eric cried out. The thing sprang at him with agility and strength beyond what it looked capable of, as though propelled through some means other than its own body. It leapt on him, landing with its hands on his chest and its feet on his knees, throwing him out of his chair and remaining on top of him once he stopped, pinning him to the ground.

Paul got himself to his feet, his back aching from the fall. When he looked up, he saw that the thing had gripped Eric's head between its skeleton hands and was lifting him by it. Then with immense force, it threw Eric's head down against the tile floor, cracking the skull. It brought it up and threw it down again— cracking it against the floor repeatedly until the head was a round, indeterminate mess of blood and hair in its hands. Then it savagely peeled the skin away from the mass and pulled away fragments of shattered bone, revealing the soft, red-gray brain still inside. It dipped its jaws into the pulpy brain matter, smeared with blood and dangling bloody, viscous strings of fluid from its toothy mouth, slurping it down, while the blood-spattered body below was still twitching its hands and feet at the suddenness and violence of its death. Then, in some sort of ecstasy or fit, the thing continued on with the remainder of the head, ripping the jaw from the skull and tearing the muscle from the bone with its teeth, great gushes of blood streaming down its jaw and neck and spurting across its face as it gorged itself on the flesh.

Paul felt about to vomit but closed up his throat to keep it down, and edged toward the door. Then he paused briefly, looking at the thing as it feasted on Eric's remains, and allowed himself to consider the reasons for this horror, this failure—but even in the instant, he knew that there had been too many variables, too much imprecision, that he had acted hastily and in desperation, and that there was no hope for an explanation. He knew, as his mind raced, that he analyzed the problem in vain, for even if he were able to discern an identifiable mistake or series of mistakes, he could not go back and rectify them. What was done was done, and he did not know why.

And yet he felt sure that there must still be something of Darcy in the figure that he observed huddled and bloodying itself over the mangled corpse of his friend and partner. He abandoned his retreat, and instead held his position, hoping to have a longer look, maybe even a closer one.

He took a step forward.

When it saw him move, the thing stopped and turned its head toward him, its face more deeply transformed than before. The decay had worsened, the eyes had clouded over with a deeper emptiness. The lower portion of the face and the rest of its contorted body was hidden in shadow and the darkness of blood. There was nothing at all recognizable in it. Paul cried out, and then he turned and ran.

He was vaguely aware of the possibility of the creature following him as he ran hastily out of the lab and down the hallway toward the stairs. He had seen its speed, and he knew that if he looked behind him, he would slow down, and his best chance to escape was to run as fast as he could. He did not know whether the creature had followed him or not.

He threw himself against the lever for the fire escape exit door. The door burst open and he stumbled into the stairwell. The fire alarm sounded, echoing loudly in the chamber. Paul clambered frantically down the stairs, and in his haste, he lost his footing around a corner and slipped. He fell almost the entire length of stairs to the next landing. His body slammed against the wall upside-down with his head pinned under it, and his neck snapped. He rocked back away from the wall, his head still pinned at an angle underneath his shoulders. He could see nothing but his own immovable legs. He could not breathe. Blotches of light exploded in his vision as he lost oxygen. After another few moments filled with no thought other than an impassive awareness of death, he suffocated. His body lay still in the position of his fall as though it were continuous and he had been frozen still in the midst of it. He never saw the dark and bloody figure looming above him; he never witnessed its slow, deliberate descent down the stairs; he never smelled its rank contagious breath as it knelt over him, and he never felt when it sank its wretched teeth into his flesh.

***

Pink fingertips of light stretched through the blue haze of the dead night in preparation for the dawn. As the quiet air expanded and the glass faces of each building glittered with distant light, a figure emerged to mock the yellow promise of the dawn—a figure neither dead nor alive, nor anywhere between, a figure of otherness, a figure of chaos. Staggering into the brightening world, it reached its skeleton hands to the sun and cried out with inhuman tones declaring its uncanny presence on earth—and the city awoke.

BREACH

The school was still under construction. Mrs. Cathy Overlee walked after her class as it descended the steps of the portable building that served as her classroom. She followed the students across what were once parking spaces on a patch of asphalt that now served as a pathway for walking between buildings. Looking to the side, she could see the partial construction of what would become a new wing to the school. At this stage, it was simply a plywood cutout skeleton. Crossing the makeshift walkway, Mrs. Overlee and her students entered the main school building. This building was undergoing renovation itself, although the end into which they walked was so far unchanged. The blue paint on the heavy metal doors was faded and peeling. The walls were scored and dirty, and the patterned mottling on the tile floor no longer camouflaged the grime as well as it used to. The fluorescent lights lining the roof hummed and clicked, although the sound was mostly drowned out by the murmur of students moving through the halls—students who seemed to be as grimy as their surroundings. There were heads of greasy hair, there were hunched shoulders wearing hand-me-down jackets and weighed down with backpacks beaten and frayed from years of use. There were faces that, although young, looked aged and worn down.

Some of them smiled, but Cathy wondered if the smiles that appeared genuine weren't smiles of malice, mischief, or arrogance. She had been a teacher for many years now, and she knew that with high-school students, appearances did not always represent the truth. These days, she was suspicious of all students except those whom she felt she knew well enough to trust. There were not many of them though, and they never smiled.

Although she had studied music and piano performance in college, Cathy was a humanities teacher, trading off between teaching English and History. She was relatively young, and she was unmarried—although, since she was over thirty, the students already categorized her nebulously as an "adult."

She knew she was getting older too because she had felt more and more aloof to her students, especially when teaching literature. Many of the students seemed unable or unwilling to identify with the characters they read about. Their main concerns with literature were mostly rationalistic and logistical (how was Gertrude able to describe Ophelia's death in such detail if she hadn't been there to witness it?). They would find and exploit unintended sexual meanings in the language of older authors. Worst of all, they would often make tragedy into a source of amusement. But Cathy did not have time to read much literature with her classes because of the short periods and ever-changing curriculum, and when she did, she usually did so with supplemental materials to guide her students' reading and thought. She had come to prefer the "canned" method to the more open-ended approach of letting the students make of the literature what they would on their own.

The masses moved from this section of the building into the next where the renovation was underway. The stale smell of the old hallway was overtaken by the smells of plywood and plaster, fresh paint and drywall. A plastic sheet was all that separated the students from some areas of construction. It always gave Cathy a twinge of anxiety to watch them pass by it, as she knew that at any moment one might breach the boundary in careless rebellion, and that she would then be responsible for the student's safety and held accountable to correct the situation.

They exited this building and walked outside again, crossing a path into what was an altogether newly constructed building. New tile glistened under their feet. White paint coated the walls evenly and cleanly. The smell of freshly milled and finished wood wafted toward them from the gymnasium.

The students—the grimy, worn-down students—took their places, looking about casually and carelessly at their new surroundings, surroundings which seemed less suited to them than the grimy, worn-down, unrenovated building they had just left.

After the student body had, for the most part, gathered and taken their places in the bleachers, the speaker for the assembly stepped forward. He was a thick-set, middle-aged man with a potbelly and a strong double chin and was clad in the uniform of a police officer. The senior class president, Hailey Rowell, stepped forward with the microphone and called the students to attention.

"Good morning," she shouted, instinctively competing with the conversations even though her voice was amplified through the PA system. A whine of feedback reverberated through the rafters. The conversational murmur subsided, but did not die. "Good morning, everybody. Can we quiet down, please?" Hailey paced authoritatively around the gym floor. The students brought their murmur to a hush in response.

"All right, thank you," she said. "Well, welcome to the annual drug and alcohol awareness assembly. We have with us Dr. Stuart Miller to talk with you all today. He has served our county as a medical examiner and has also worked for the coroner's office. Now he is an investigator for the sheriff. He is also a proud parent of one of your fellow Wildcats, Brooke Miller. But before we start, let's all observe a moment of silence for the tragedy that happened in Sacramento yesterday."

As Hailey had taken the floor, the students had still been murmuring amongst themselves, but at her request, their conversations died out completely.

There had been a school shooting in Sacramento. From what Cathy had tried to intuit of her students that morning, it hadn't seemed to affect them much; they had seemed the same. And right now, during the moment of silence, she could not tell whether the silence was truly respectful or merely apathetic. Mrs. Overlee was conscious of the gun in Dr. Miller's holster and was not sure how she felt about it, or how she should have felt.

"Thank you," Hailey said. "Now, let's have a round of applause for our speaker, Dr. Miller." She clapped her free hand against the hand that was holding the microphone, sending a loud series of pops through the amplification system in the gym. The gathered students followed suit and clapped as Dr. Miller took the microphone.

In a tone that was firm and business-like, he spoke articulately about his work and relayed his knowledge about drugs and alcohol in a way that was easily understandable but not condescending. He described the chemical properties of certain drugs and explained the effects they had, especially focusing on the toll each exacted on the human body when used long-term. As he continued to speak, he seemed to grow more comfortable; his tone became less formal and more direct.

"So, let's face it," he said, toward the end of his speech. "You use any of these drugs, even the ones that are 'not that bad'—which, trust me, they are all 'that bad'—you lose control of yourself, you wind up addicted, you end up losing your teeth, your lungs, your friends… and worst of all, your own life. If it's not the drug that kills you, it might be your own vomit when you get too wasted to know up from down, a house fire when you got lazy and dropped your blunt on the floor. There's any number of ways that a drug can kill you other than the actual drug itself. The drug wants you dead and it doesn't care how it does it. The point is, you will die. You will die, you will die, you will die. And for what? What did you leave behind? You will have left behind a legacy—a legacy of loss. A legacy of bad decisions, a legacy of disappointments, a legacy of other people taking care of you because you won't be able to take care of yourself, and finally, a legacy of life lost for no good reason at all.

"And you will lose the most important thing of all: *yourself*. You will lose your chance at truly finding yourself, and being yourself in the most fulfilling way. You will lose your chance at following your passions and achieving your dreams. The future is yours, if you make the right decisions. You're in control. It's up to you."

The finality of his cadence prompted applause.

"Any questions?" Dr. Miller asked once the applause had died down.

The students murmured quietly, and before long, a hand went up.

"Yes," Dr. Miller said, holding the microphone out to the distant bleacher although there was no hope of the microphone picking up the student's voice.

"How long have you been a medical examiner?"

"Fif*teen* years, and I've performed more autopsies than I can even count at this point. It's sad. It's real sad."

Another question.

"Yes."

"What's the worst thing you've ever seen?"

There was some sniggering from the crowd, but Dr. Miller indulged the question.

"Worst thing I ever saw—well, other than families being torn apart, the havoc wrought on kids and relationships… Once I had to examine a man whose arm had *rotted off* because he had done so much heroin. It was still attached to him, but it had gotten so bad that the whole arm was dead—all black and rotten. It was still attached to him. We had to take it off. That's probably the most *memorable* thing I've seen. So that's an example to you of how bad things can actually get. His arm was *dead*."

Another question.

"Yes."

"What is the most dangerous drug? Or, I mean, what's the worst drug in your opinion?"

"The *worst* drug? Marijuana."

A murmuring wave of mild incredulity swept through the bleachers.

"Well, let's face it," Dr. Miller continued. "Like I said, sometimes the drug itself won't kill you, and as far as that goes, it's not as likely that marijuana itself will kill you as it is that some other drug would, like cocaine or heroin. But nobody wakes up after never having done any drug ever and says, 'I think I'll try heroin today.' No. I say marijuana is the most dangerous because it affects your judgement, and when you lose your judgement, you start making other stupid decisions that *will* kill you—and also because it's most people's gateway drug, and it's *real* easy to get hooked on needing to find a bigger, better fix after you start to get bored."

Another hand.

"Yes."

"My whole family smokes marijuana and they're fine. They're normal."

More tense sniggers rippled through the crowd. Dr. Miller remained serious.

"Trust me, they're not fine. They're not normal. They may be normal to *you*. But trust me, they're not normal. Normal is relative, like everything. It all depends on your context. You might look at them and think, 'Hey, that's normal.' But I might look at them and think, 'Whoa, there is something definitely wrong here!' Maybe your family's normal isn't what you should be shooting for. It might be that what's 'normal' for your family might actually be something that holds you back. Don't give up on the chance to really achieve your dreams. Don't give up on the opportunity to really be yourself—without drugs."

By this time, the noise in the bleachers had increased considerably, students talking freely with one another at a conversational volume. Hailey took the microphone back. "Thank you, Dr. Miller. That's all the time we have. It's time to get to your third period class! Have a great day, Wildcats!"

As the students filed out, Cathy heard a conversation between two students who were walking behind her.

"Weed is not the most dangerous drug," a boy said.

"Clearly not," said a second. "But," he added sarcastically, "you won't achieve your dreams if you smoke weed? What? I know successful people smoke weed."

"What if my dream is just to smoke a lot of weed? What if *that's* my dream? What if my dream is to die from smoking weed because all I want to do is smoke weed and die happy?"

They laughed. Cathy was disgusted. She turned around to face them and stopped them abruptly. She did not recognize them; at least, she had not had them in class before. They looked at her, stunned, caught.

"Boys," she said curtly. "You know that your life is important—you are important. You have one life to live, so make sure you live it right—live the way you will want to have lived. Don't waste it!"

The boys nodded and muttered some words that indicated assent. Somewhat satisfied, Mrs. Overlee directed them to go to class.

***

The school was located just outside the heart of a small northwest town, surrounded by woods. The close quarters of the school belied the expanse and the sparseness of the area that it served. Cathy worked out of a portable at one end of the main grounds of the school. The original building was immediately next to her portable. Beyond that were the new, completed gymnasium, auditorium, and office spaces. In front of all of these was the new construction, which was taking place in what used to be the parking lot. In the meantime, teachers parked on what used to be a field immediately in front of the school. This added to the already cramped feeling lent by the overloaded classrooms and tight hallways.

Third period was Cathy's planning period. Before returning to her classroom, she went to the workroom that adjoined the main office in the finished new construction. From her mailbox, she retrieved some copies that had been made by her teacher assistant. They were half-sheet rubrics, meant to be cut in order to save paper. The rubrics were not really necessary since she had already given the students their assignment and requirements, and the project was due at the end of the school year and would not be returned to them. But she had had the copies made anyway.

The workroom's paper cutter was a relic from the 70s, when the original school had been constructed. The blade was made of heavy metal, probably iron. It had recently been sharpened after decades of continuous use had worn the blade dull. Now it cut cleanly through thick stacks. There was some worry that the sharpness of the blade posed a hazard—one teacher had already cut her finger on it—but the administration did not take this seriously.

She placed the stack on the board, aligned it, and brought down the weighty blade with a resounding *ka-chunk!*

She collected the cut papers in her hand and left the office. All of the students were in class and the hallways were quiet. If she had not been able to peer into the windows to confirm that classes were in session, she might have thought that the school was empty. She returned to her classroom, opened the door, and, to her great surprise, found it already occupied by a student. Then she remembered that she had arranged a meeting. It had slipped her mind after the assembly.

The student's name was Sara Unterman. She was a senior, short, but very beautiful. She had gotten pregnant near the beginning of the school year, presumably at a Halloween party, so went the rumors around the school. Now it was nearing the end of the school year, and there was no mistaking that she was due soon. (She couldn't have timed it better, Cathy thought ironically.) Sara's situation necessitated special accommodations, academic and otherwise. Most of the classrooms at the school had desks with chairs fixed to them, and since Sara could not fit in the desks anymore, she had to arrange for special seating. In Cathy's classroom, she used a worktable at the back of the room as her desk and sat on a plastic orange chair that, more likely than not, was as old as the paper cutter.

It was Sara's lunch hour, and she had come in to ask for help on an assignment. She was standing at the back of the classroom looking at a poster print of fractal designs, a hand-me-down from the teacher who had used the classroom before Cathy. It was the least interesting of the posters in the room, Cathy thought, or at least the least inspiring. She had adorned her room with many motivational posters. One of these read, "Dream, Believe, Achieve!" Another said, "What is your message to the world?" A third, probably her favorite: "Don't change so people will like you. Be yourself and the right people will love the real you." Some others said, "Live life to the fullest," "Star in your own life," "If you never try, you'll never know," "Mistakes are forgivable… so long as you learn from them!" and "Your decisions affect your future." There were more in addition to these. The one poster in her room with the largest writing of all said, in bold caps, NO CELL PHONES ALLOWED—although, of course, this was meant to be motivational in a different sense from the others.

At Cathy's entrance, Sara turned around and smiled from the side, her pregnant belly bulging in profile.

"Hi, Mrs. Overlee," she said.

"Hello, Sara. I had forgotten that you were coming. I hope you weren't waiting too long."

"No, I just got here."

Cathy smiled as she took her seat at her desk. Sara walked from the back of the room through the rows of desks toward her.

"I was wondering if I could come in some time to get help on the final project. I'm still a little confused on it."

Cathy flashed a smile at her again. "Well, we are getting pretty close to the end of the school year. What was it that you needed help on? Maybe I could answer your question right now."

Sara leaned back against one of the desks, half-sitting, half-standing, and setting her book bag on the floor next to her, her belly bulging out in a way that struck Cathy as almost ostentatious.

"Well, it's not so much a question, really. I just was wondering if I could get your help on it. I could come in after school, or maybe before school. My mom drives me."

"Well, it's getting pretty close to the end of the school year."

"How late are you here after school? I can stay after school."

"I wish you had come to me about this sooner." Cathy smiled again.

"I did—I asked you if you could help me when you handed out the assignment, and you said to talk to you the next week. Today is Monday, so here I am."

"Well, I admire your dedication," Cathy said at last. "You are certainly setting yourself up with successful habits for the future." She smiled encouragingly.

Sara shrugged and smiled shyly. "My life is going to be a little bit more complicated after I graduate. I'm just trying to be prepared."

"Very wise. I want you to know, I think that what you're doing is very brave, and I support you in whatever you decide."

"Thanks. I just want to make sure to do whatever is best for my baby. I need to make sure that I graduate. I want to make sure I meet the requirements."

"Oh, I'm sure you will. Focusing on your education will make you more successful, and will make you a better parent. It will help you give the baby a better foundation financially and emotionally."

"Well, thanks for being willing to help. I really appreciate it."

"Of course, of course. Now, what was it that you needed help with? I mean, what was your question?"

"I don't really have a specific question. I just need help getting started, basically." She rummaged around in her book bag. "I don't really know what to write about." She pulled out the paper for the assignment that Cathy had given to the class, a front-and-back copy of instructions, suggested procedures, grading policies, due dates, and a sampling of potential topics. She turned it over in her hands as though looking for something other than text—other than the paper itself. "I'm just not really sure what I'm supposed to do."

"Well," Mrs. Overlee said, trying not to let the strain show through her voice. "It's a personal response prompt. The assignment is for you to find something in your personal life to talk about in connection the prompt. That's something I can't really help you with, since I don't know as much about your personal life as you! Just be authentic. Show me who you really are. Express yourself!"

Somewhat to Cathy's surprise, Sara's face expressed disappointment and resignation—as though she had suspected that Cathy would give exactly the answer that she had given, but had still hoped for something entirely different. Cathy could not imagine what sort of answer Sara was hoping to find.

"I just don't think about much else except for the baby right now," Sara said at last, with a tired smile.

"Then write about the baby!"

"But the baby isn't myself. This assignment asks me to write about myself."

"Then write about how you feel about the baby."

Sara gave exactly the same expression she had given earlier, and then she appeared to give up.

"All right, I'll try. Can I still come in after school sometime, maybe?" she asked, sliding the paper back into her backpack.

"Yes," said Cathy hesitantly. "I should be here after school… pretty much any day of the week this week. Just check with me on the day of to make sure. But I think I'll be around."

"Would Wednesday work?"

"Okay," Cathy relented. "Check in with me on Wednesday."

"Great. Thank you, Mrs. Overlee," said Sara, standing. She threw her book bag over her shoulder with an agility that Cathy marked as uncommon for a woman so pregnant and attributed it to her youth. Sara walked out of the room, her feet plodding on the floor—but she held her head high. Despite her plodding gait, the air about her was so light that Cathy would not have been surprised to see her skipping instead of walking.

As soon as she had left, Cathy leaned back in her desk chair and sighed. She had meant what she had said to Sara—that she admired her courage. No one would argue that it didn't take guts to finish out senior year of high school pregnant, not only passing classes but excelling in them, putting forward the effort to really do well. But something about Sara rubbed Cathy the wrong way. As Sara rounded the corner out of the doorframe and started down the steps, she took a moment to try to pinpoint what it was.

Cathy Overlee was not old. But she was old enough to have made mistakes in her youth, to have made the tough decisions and to have dealt with the consequences. She had not been much older than Sara when she had had an abortion. It was not something that she was proud of—having gotten pregnant by mistake—and having the abortion seemed to have been the least of all possible evils. She did not know what might have lain in store of her had she decided instead to carry the baby—but as she looked back, she could see that having the abortion had given her the opportunity to finish pursuing her career in education, and because of that, she was able to help teach and mentor so many youths, and to find fulfillment and achieve her personal dream, which had always been to become a teacher. It had been difficult, yes, and the failures had been many, but her successes were so valuable to her that it was as though they were a part of her, as much as her hands and arms were of her physical body.

But despite these successes, and despite having made peace about the abortion, doubts continued to nag at her. Cathy had studied piano performance as an undergraduate, and although she hated to admit it, she had dreamed of being a professional performer as much as becoming a teacher. The hope, of course, seemed more and more distant as the years flew by, but she would often drum on her desk with her fingers, practicing with her hands alone to keep herself in shape should the opportunity present itself to reenter her musical life. Her hands were wiry and bony. She would often look at the ugly things and think to herself, they were once—and should be still—such tools of beauty... but now they were being wasted...

When Sara had gotten pregnant, Cathy had thought to herself that aborting the baby would have been a smarter choice, but she hadn't wanted to get in the way of Sara's choices, which she respected even if she didn't agree. Anyway, she had not been on personal enough terms with Sara to make a recommendation either way. She was still not on very personal terms with her. But she wanted to be, if only to share her own life story with the hope that it might inspire Sara and enable her to find greater fulfillment later in life, perhaps even greater fulfillment than herself.

Her thoughts were interrupted as the intercom speaker, positioned directly above her desk, buzzed to direct attention.

"May I have your attention please," came a male voice over the intercom. "This is Principal Connolly. May I have your attention immediately. We are now going into lockdown mode. This is not a drill. I repeat, this is not a drill. We are going into lockdown mode. Teachers, lock your doors and draw your blinds. Please listen for further announcements."

Cathy's heart leapt at the announcement. She did not have a class in her room at the moment, which relieved a little of her anxiety. But then, she remembered Sara.

She ran to the door and opened it. Sara was still outside on the walkway.

"Sara!" Cathy called.

At that moment, she looked in the direction of the construction site. She saw that the construction workers had stopped work, and were walking together en masse toward the school. They were not running, which seemed somewhat reassuring. There was clearly no imminent threat. Her mind raced with the potentialities: a bomb threat? A threat against a student? An escaped convict in the general area? (They were near a women's correctional facility.)

Cathy beckoned to Sara with her hand. "Come on inside, quickly."

Sara stepped quickly up the stairs and into the classroom. Cathy closed and locked the door behind her.

"What's going on?" asked Sara.

"I don't know."

Cathy drew down the venetian blinds and closed them, darkening the room.

Sara instinctively took her place at the back of the room, in the orange chair that had been specially designated for her. After closing the blinds, Cathy headed back to her desk and sat. She smiled up at Sara, who smiled back, clearly anxious. Cathy was anxious too, but she turned to the work she had in front of her, scoring essays where she had left off. More than likely, the lockdown was just something they would have to wait out—a bomb scare, or something like it.

She had not gotten far before there was a loud thump. She looked up at Sara. Sara had started in surprise and turned around— the noise had seemed to come from outside, behind her. It had sounded to Cathy like something striking the window—a bird, maybe, or someone bumping into it. She had heard the noise before, from students bumping into it carelessly as they walked by the portable. It seemed louder to her now, but she guessed that it was due to her anxiety.

Sara was pale. She looked alternately at Cathy and behind herself, at the blinded windows.

Cathy said, "We can't look out. During a lockdown, we're supposed to have the windows blocked."

There was another loud thump. Sara looked at Cathy almost imploringly. Cathy gestured back to her with raised, open palms and a shrug. *What can I do?*

Another thump.

Sara grew even more pale, and her eyes began to water.

Cathy finally rose from her desk and crossed the room, observing that she could have reduced their distance to each other sooner.

As she approached, she heard another noise: a low murmuring sound, like human voices but with an animal quality, and then she understood why Sara's fear had appeared more extreme than the situation called for. From the other side of the room, Cathy had not heard the noises.

Then came another thump, and this time, there was no doubt that something was striking against the window.

Cathy stood and Sara sat motionless, both of them staring at the blinds, transfixed at the strange murmuring sound that came from behind them. Cathy had to fight an intense urge to pry open the blinds and look out. She turned and looked at the intercom, although she knew that looking would do no good. She looked at the clock to its side. It told the time.

Cathy drew closer to Sara and sat lightly on the edge of Sara's table.

The glass thumped again, this time seemingly right before their staring faces, so loud and forceful that it made them both flinch.

Then, her head clearing for a moment, Cathy thought, they should get away from the windows. They should get as far away as they possibly could, to the opposite side of the room, and shelter themselves however they might.

But yet she had no idea what was on the other side of the window. Perhaps there were people outside—the construction workers, maybe. Maybe they needed shelter, and they were pounding on the windows to be let in.

Then there was the fact that she didn't know either way what was outside those windows. What had she to fear? Yes, that was it. A being can only fear a thing it knows, and she did not know what was outside of the room, so she deduced that she was actually afraid of something she was making up in her head, some sort of abstraction to fill in the void of knowledge. If she reacted in fear before knowing all the facts, that would not be sensible, nor would it align with how she wanted to live her life. She didn't wish to live in fear, to be controlled by it. She desired to live her life freely. She decided that she would look. She would look because she refused to be controlled by fear.

She motioned for Sara to keep her place and remain calm by gesturing with the display of her open hand. Sara looked bewildered.

Cathy moved closer to the blinds, gently put her finger to it, and pushed it up, opening a slit through which she glimpsed—

But the sight was so terrifying that she was not even sure of what she had seen. She fell back and collapsed on the floor. The image flashed through her mind repeatedly, distorted and grotesque.

Sara looked down at Cathy collapsed in a heap on the floor when suddenly something struck the window again, this time breaking the glass and bursting through. The venetian blinds rattled and a hand reached through—a blueing, mottled hand, fingers arched and clutching outward, muscles tensed and trembling violently.

Sara toppled off of her chair. The desk pushed forward, and Sara dropped to the floor. Fragments of shattered glass littered the floor around her and flecked her hair and clothes like jewels.

Then, in rapid succession, the other windows broke. The blinds shook and other hands reached through, all desperately clutching the air before them. The murmur of voices had ascended to an agitated chorus of growls and moans.

The blinds shook and bulged—they were trying to climb in, to find their way through the narrow frames.

Cathy screamed and grabbed at Sara's arm, taking hold of her wrist, and pulled her away from the windows with all her strength.

Sara assisted by crawling on her knees until she had drawn herself beyond the table. Cathy tipped the table over on its side. It was too narrow to cover the windows at all.

"Stay out!" Cathy shouted. She grabbed a desk and attempted to brace it against the window, but the writhing hands abruptly pushed it back. She fell again, the desk rolling over her and landing upside-down on the floor.

Sara had crawled back toward the window. She grabbed the table and pulled it upright again. Cathy got up, picked up the desk, and laid it on its side on top of the table. Another push from the hands slid the desk back on the surface of the table, nearly knocking it off. In desperation, Cathy laid her hands on a heavy metal cabinet against the wall next to the row of windows and pitched it forward. It landed with a resounding thud against the edge of the table, textbooks and notebooks toppling over heavily within it. The impact threw the desk off of the table, and the cabinet came to rest at an angle, leaning against the edge of the table. The hands from outside banged against the metal loudly, but the heavy cabinet did not move. Cathy then turned and grabbed another desk, moved it quickly against the cabinet, hoping that the extra weight might provide a little more resistance. Sara did the same, sliding one desk and then another against the angled metal cabinet. The pounding grew louder and more rapid, but the cabinet held.

Adjoining the classroom was a storage closet with books. Cathy indicated it.

"In there," she said.

Sara shook her head violently, her face pale and sweating. Her lips were lighter than her face.

"Come on. It's safer in there. They might get through."

Sara shook her head, this time with an intensity that rattled through her body in a shiver. "Claustrophobic," she said.

Cathy grimaced but conceded. She put her hand on Sara's shoulder in a gesture of consolation.

Sara looked up at her with complete fear in her eyes. The metallic pounding persisted.

Then Sara grimaced.

"Oh my God," she said. "Oh my God."

Cathy withdrew her hand as though her touch were responsible for the outcry.

"What is it?" Cathy asked, even though she already had an idea.

"That was a contraction… I think it was a contraction…"

Cathy held out her hands to put them on her shoulders again, but stopped midway through the gesture and abandoned it.

"What can I do?" she asked.

"I don't know!" Sara said, her voice straining. She grimaced and bent over again. She backed away and got on her hands and knees, hanging her head between her arms. She exhaled in relief as the contraction passed.

The hands pounded relentlessly on the metal cabinet. The door rattled.

Sara moaned, a deep, resonant, animal-like howl, and pitched her back down at an angle, her rear in the air, her hands stretched before her.

Cathy had been wringing her hands, and as she realized what she had been doing, she clutched each hand with the other to stop the absurd, useless motion.

Sara put her head on the floor when the contraction had finished, and breathed deeply. "It hurts," she said. "It hurts… Oh my God…"

She rolled onto her back with what appeared to be great effort. Grimacing, she bent one leg up toward her and stretched her arm downward to remove her shoe. Cathy rushed to her aid and quickly removed the other shoe. Sara pulled her shirt over her mountainous belly and slid her pants down from her waist. Cathy assisted her, pulling the pants down and removing them. She looked about her classroom for anything that might be of assistance to them, but she did not really know what to look for.

The carpet was rough and dirty, digging into Cathy's hand as she knelt to assist Sara, particles of dirt clinging to her sweating palm. She got up and went to the wall and began removing the posters from all around the room. She began with the fractal designs, and then moved on to the others—"Live life to the fullest"—"Star in your own life"—"Mistakes are forgivable"—

She brought them to where Sara was and spread them out on the floor, overlapping the edges so that they formed something of a smooth, clean surface. She wrapped her arm around the small of Sara's back and assisted her, crawling, to the posters.

Another contraction came, and Sara writhed on the floor, now on her side, but this time, instead of a low moan, she emitted a terrible, high-pitched scream. Her breathing came faster. When the contraction had finished, she looked with terrified eyes darting aimlessly around the room. "Oh my God…"

Cathy rubbed her upper back in small, quick circles. "That's it," she said helpfully. "You're doing great…"

The beating at the cabinet had only grown stronger, and the door still rattled. But now it seemed that the hands were beating all around the portable, not just at the windows—the thuds reverberated through every wall, filling the air with the sound of their pounding. Cathy realized at this point that whomever or whatever they were, they were never going to stop.

Sara emitted an abrupt scream as clear fluid gushed out of her.

"I think that was your water breaking," Cathy said. "You're getting there. You're doing great."

Sara's breathing had continued to quicken. She took in short panting breaths like a dog, vocalizing a little on each exhalation. The vocalizations crescendoed into louder screams, and her body began to writhe violently.

"Oh my God, it hurts so much…" she said.

Blood oozed onto the posters, sliding over the slick surface.

Sara began to writhe almost uncontrollably. Cathy quickened the motion of her hand on Sara's back, although Sara's writhing made it difficult to keep her hand on it. Cathy shushed her.

Finally, Sara stopped. Through grit teeth, she screamed more loudly than she had yet. Her face flushed deep red and her eyes squeezed shut, tears rolling out of them. Cathy looked down and saw what appeared to be a sliver of the crown of the baby's head.

"I can see the baby, Sara! I can see the baby!"

Sara stopped and looked at her, her dilated eyes bleary and bloodshot. "Really?" she panted.

"Yes, I can see it!"

Sara rolled onto her back, propping herself up by her arms. She screamed again. From Sara's new position, Cathy could see the muscles clench in her belly. Sara's arms shook, and her body trembled. The crown of the baby's head seemed hardly to move at all. The blood was dripping steadily. It had flowed off of the posters and was pooling onto the carpet nearby.

"You're doing great," Cathy said.

Sara contracted again, immediately following on the previous one. She dropped back onto her elbows, pitched her head back, and screamed again. The baby's head remained the same—in fact, to Cathy, it seemed almost to have shrunk in size.

"You're doing great," she said again.

Sara rolled onto her side, launching into another contraction. The flow of blood had increased from a steady drip to something more like a stream. The stain on the carpet had spread considerably. The amount was alarming. But Cathy knew that she shouldn't say anything, so she continued to be encouraging.

"You're doing great."

Sara was exhausted and lay on the ground as though asleep. Cathy would have thought she were dead if it weren't for her breathing. She looked pale again, although now some red blotches from burst vessels stood out on her face.

The pounding on the walls, the door, and the cabinet continued, but Sara seemed entirely unaware in her exhaustion. In the lull, Cathy realized that she was trembling all over.

Then Sara seemed to awaken and threw herself into another contraction.

"That's it," Cathy said. "Push."

At this encouragement, Sara clenched her teeth together and squeezed her eyes shut. She bellowed with the contraction, the force and volume of it shocking to Cathy. The baby's head moved forward very slowly, despite the tremendous force with which Sara was pushing it outward.

Then suddenly, in the middle of the contraction, Sara yelped again with the same high-pitched scream as before and recoiled as if at some sudden, stabbing pain or shock. Cathy looked at her, bewildered.

"You're doing great," she said.

Sara shook her head. "No," she said. "No. It's not working. There's something wrong."

She collapsed, again assuming the appearance of sleep.

Cathy looked down. The crown had receded, now a barely perceptible sliver of flesh.

The pounding all around the room continued. Moans and growls filtered in through the windows and the walls.

Sara lay on the floor motionless for a long time. Cathy finally reached out to her, shook her gently by the shoulder, and said, "Come on, Sara. You can do it."

Sara only shook her head in response, her eyes still closed. "It hurts too much. I can't do it. There's something wrong."

"There's nothing wrong with you. You're doing great. Come on. You can do it."

Sara weakly opened her eyes and peered up at Cathy from the red slits. She closed them again and said, "Okay."

They waited. Then another contraction came, and Cathy said, "Go for it. Do it."

Sara bellowed and screamed. Her face flushed again. The crown of the head, smeared in blood, moved forward.

"Go, go, go—" shouted Cathy.

The contraction subsided, but the head had moved forward considerably.

"You're almost there," Cathy said.

Another contraction followed, and Sara screamed and arched. The blood nearly squirted this time, and the head moved forward more quickly than it had earlier.

"You're doing it!"

The full crown cleared the opening. But then Cathy grew confused as she did not see any facial features, but only a fold of skin.

Then she realized that what she had seen was not the crown of the baby's head, but its bottom. The baby was breech.

"I can't…" Sara panted. As soon as she had breathed the words, another contraction struck.

The baby's buttocks emerged, along with the crease of skin where the legs joined and folded up. In desperation, Cathy grabbed hold with her fingers in the creases and pulled gently. The pulling seemed to help urge the baby forward, so she continued to pull, and said, "Push! I've got it!"

Sara yelled and arched back as the baby slid gradually out. The feet finally emerged and fell free, and Cathy saw that it was a boy. With another contraction, the remainder of the body emerged, and the baby lay out in the open up to its neck. Its head was still inside. The body was purple-blue and motionless.

Sara collapsed again in rest and lay back, eyes closed.

All the while, the pounding had only grown louder. The blood had pooled on the poster where Cathy knelt, and her knees and legs were soaked in it.

Sara strained with another contraction. This one seemed weaker than before, and Cathy assisted again by pulling on the baby's body. The neck emerged, along with the deep purple umbilical cord, which was wrapped around the baby's neck.

Sara heaved and vomited. The contraction subsided, but the baby's head had cleared enough for Cathy to pull it free. The head dropped lightly onto the blood-covered poster paper. Cathy fell back and let go of the legs, and the baby lay motionless.

Sara had collapsed back onto the floor, the side of her face glistening with vomit. There was no motion.

"Sara," called Cathy.

Sara did not stir. Cathy looked for evidence of her breathing but saw none. She reached up and felt her pulse with her blood-covered fingers—there was none. She withdrew her hand and sat back and looked at the baby. It was still purple-blue, motionless, the cord wrapped tightly around its neck. It too was dead.

For a moment, Cathy stared blankly at the two bodies. Then she shivered and convulsed and she screamed in horror and flung herself down on the floor.

"God, why did you *pull* on it? Why did you have to *pull* it?" Cathy screamed. "Oh, God, God!"

She held up her hands—her ugly, bony hands—and they were covered with blood.

Suddenly, the metal cabinet slid off of the edge of the table and fell to the floor with a loud crash. The venetian blinds tore from the window frames.

Cathy screamed, jumped up, and bolted for the book closet. She threw open the door, leapt inside just as she could feel cold fingers at her back, her hair, her neck—and slammed the door shut behind her.

***

She awoke with a start. All was quiet, and all was dark. She became aware of her body first. She was aware of a layer of sweat, of stink. As she began to move, her muscles resisted, exhausted from some strain. The sleep had been good. For a moment, she closed her eyes in the darkness and let the feeling of fatigue cascade over her like waves of lukewarm water. Her head throbbed gently.

Then everything came back to her in a sudden wave: Sara, the birth, the baby, death, death, everything death, and the hideous creatures climbing in through the windows.

Her heart quickened in fear at the fresh memories and her eyes bolted open, although the only thing that greeted them was the darkness.

Then, at last, she remembered where she was. She was in the book closet, a small carpeted space, walls lined with books that absorbed and deadened sound and muted the scuffling she made as she scrambled up to her knees. It was like a tomb.

She felt along the walls and found the one with the door, and she felt the bare wall next to it, reaching up for the light switch. She turned on the light. The light was intense and blinding for a moment, but her eyes soon adjusted.

She put her ear to the door and listened closely for a moment. She could not distinguish any noise coming from outside the door. She could not be certain—the movement of pressing her ear against the door and the thudding of her own heart and the static of her own ears in the silence of the room seemed like a cacophony, and within it, she thought she heard all sorts of monstrous scufflings and growlings from without.

She sat back for a while in the blaring, terrifying silence. She knew that sooner or later she would have to open the door. Would it make a difference how long she waited? If they were waiting for her outside the door, they would wait as long as she could, for all she knew. If they weren't waiting, then she was wasting time.

She reached up to the handle. She lost her balance momentarily and she swung her hand down to maintain balance, unintentionally hitting the door handle. The impact made a loud bang which, in the room full of books, died out as though it had never happened.

She waited a moment, her ear close to the door. As before, she could discern no sound.

She sat back. She waited.

Then she wiped her hands on her pants and reached up again at the handle, this time very carefully. She put her hand to it and turned it gently, making no noise. She turned it until it stopped, and then she pushed it outward just as slowly. A sliver of light from the classroom appeared. She looked up and down it, seeing nothing. She pushed the door a little more, silently. When nothing happened, she swung it gently open all the way, revealing the entire classroom to her view.

The blinds had been torn completely from the windows. All of the glass had been broken in, so the row of windows opened to the air outside. The smell was of fresh spring in late afternoon. Pure sunlight fell through and lit on the metal cabinet, the overturned desks, and the old carpet.

Slowly, Cathy stood and entered the room. She had only taken one step when she stopped again—on the floor lay the strangled baby, dry, blue, and lifeless, its eyes closed. It was stone dead. The skin was dry now, but still blue in color. The cord was still around its neck, and nearby, attached to the other end of the cord, was the uterus. Sara was nowhere to be seen.

Strange, thought Cathy.

Something compelled her to draw closer to the baby. She looked long and hard at its shriveled, naked, grotesque body. She felt that she should weep but she could not. Although she had not wept at all, she felt empty, as though she had been weeping for hours. All she could do was look at it for a long time, as though the length of her looking would compensate for her lack of tears. Then she looked out the empty windows, through the sunlight, into the air that was more silent than she could remember.

She walked away from the dead infant, going between the rows of undisturbed desks toward the door and windows, through the maze of overturned desks and spilled books, and over Sara's table, which lay on its side again.

She had neither seen nor heard anything out of the ordinary, so she was less cautious now. She opened the door to the classroom gently and stepped out into the warm open air. The trees rustled slightly in the wind, and birds sang. There was no other sound or motion, as though the school was abandoned—or still in session. Now that she was out of the room and no longer looking at the direct evidence of the carnage, she half expected to find that she had imagined it all and that the students and teachers were all still inside the building, going about their business as usual. But there was always some bustle or other outside when school was in session—a student being dropped off or picked up, a teacher in their planning period moving from building to building, or students running errands. The quiet was uncanny.

She walked out onto the landing and down the steps, to the asphalt below. Her footsteps sounded lightly on the ground. She looked up at the construction site that stood boldly and nakedly in the sun. Beyond the building, she could see all of the cars parked in their spaces, like inert, bejeweled insects glistening in the sun.

She walked into the shade cast by the main building and stepped up to the door. Once at the door, she listened, but as before, she heard nothing. She grabbed the handle and pulled the heavy door open.

Inside, the hallway was dark, silent, and empty. The lights had either been turned off or gone out; the only light came from the skylight far above, partially shaded by trees that moved gently in the wind.

After a moment, she stepped forward. Her foot plopped into something slippery and wet, and she almost lost her balance. She braced herself against the doorframe. Once she had regained her balance, she looked down.

Her shoe had landed in blood at least an inch deep. She looked ahead. The thick blood covered the tile floor evenly down the entire hallway, deep red and glistening like a dark, glossy polish, shadows passing unevenly down the surface as the wind played at the trees outside. Black lumps of debris lay scattered down the hallway, half-submerged.

The feeling of dread returned to her. She brought her other foot down into the liquid and let the door close behind her. She walked forward, cautious not to lose her balance, or to make much noise, or to disturb the blood so greatly that it would splash. As she walked down the hallway, she inspected the pieces of debris: books, pieces of food, articles of clothing—and body parts, some recognizable as fingers, hands, pieces of arms, legs, others organs or flesh-covered remains mangled beyond recognition. Her throat caught. She had become conscious of the smell of it, the metallic smell of blood, and the stench of decay as of old, warm meat. Blood coated the bottom of the lockers and had splattered up to the tops, in some cases reaching the bare walls and the molding above them.

She noticed features of the hallway that she hadn't before. She noticed the height of the ceiling, almost church-like. She noticed the painted murals, how lifeless their cartoonish designs were, and how even more garish they were now in the dark and spattered with blood. It was as though she were really seeing the halls for the first time.

As she walked down the hall, she peered into the windows of the adjoining classrooms. Many of the windows were smeared with blood. The classrooms into which she could look were dark— no lights, empty.

There were no remains in the classrooms that she could see, save for the odd piece of debris, as were scattered throughout the hall. It was not nearly enough to account for all of the students. Where had everyone gone?

She continued down the hall, stepping delicately through the blood. At the throat of the hallway was a junction to the library on the left, the main office just beyond, the other classrooms and the gymnasium ahead, and the main entrance on the right. She lingered to look in at the library. It too was unlit. She could make out larger, darker forms that appeared to be intact bodies— although the scarcity of light made them seem twisted, or heaped in odd positions that barely resembled human forms.

Curious about these, she walked closer and put her face up to the window. Looking in, she could not make out anything more clearly than she already had. It was all still very dark and obscure.

She tried the handle; the door was unlocked. She pulled at the door. It was sticky with blood and she had to pull hard to release it from the jamb.

The library carpet was soaked in blood. It squished under her feet as she walked in. The door thudded behind her.

She looked down at the nearest form.

It was a human body. The legs ended in darkness, bent out of view or torn off or destroyed. One arm was twisted behind at an unnatural angle, as though it had been pulled out of its socket, and the other presumably lay under the body. The back of the head was gone from just above the neck, the skull hollowed out, only some indeterminate mass and liquid pooled behind where the face was or used to be.

Cathy was about to cry out, when she looked up and saw a form at some distance from her, standing at the other end of the rows of bookshelves. It was a person, but in the darkness, she couldn't make out who it was.

She moved toward the person. After her motion seemed to generate no response, she presumed the person was facing away from her, toward the wall or the ground.

"Hello?" she called out.

The figure turned abruptly, revealing a face that seemed itself to emerge out of darkness from the bottom, save for eyes that glared out from underneath a drawn brow with a glimmer as though they were lit from within. They had a hollow stare, akin to what Cathy had glimpsed between the blinds and through the window of her own classroom not long ago, although seeing it for the second time seemed to terrify her more—its repetition was the confirmation of its existence.

The eyes leapt out of the darkness at her with the rest of the shadowy form, and at the next moment, it was upon her, its fingers around her throat and its teeth flashing out of a black, decaying face. Then she became aware that there were two of them—she was not sure where the other had come from, or that it hadn't been two all along.

Three of them pulled at her clothes, her wrists, her hair, her neck, until four of them had managed to pin her to the floor. She kicked wildly, throwing one of them back against a bookshelf. Just as another lunged for her, its mouth opening wide as though it wanted to swallow her entire face, another body thrust itself against her face, knocking her out of the way. She kicked at it and it rolled into the others, knocking them down.

The figure stood. It had a gun in its hand. It took aim quickly and fired three shots in succession. The first two struck two of the creatures, one in the shoulder, sending it recoiling backwards, and the second in the face of the second, tossing its head back and sending up a spray of black liquid. The third appeared to be a miss, for the third creature continued its advance and leapt at the figure. There was a brief tussle on the floor, and then two shots in rapid succession, and a warm spray, and the smell of gunpowder.

Then there was a firm hand on her arm, pulling her away. More of the creatures leapt out of the darkness of the library. She pushed at the slick, soggy carpet with her shoe and scrambled out of the library, her arm still being pulled by the stranger.

The library door slammed shut behind them. The stranger, whom she could now see more clearly in the light of the hallway, was a tall, broad man wearing dark clothing. The man slid a tire iron between the handles to the library just as one of the creatures hurled itself against it. The doors burst out from the frame, but were held together by the iron. The man turned towards her, and she saw that it was Dr. Stuart Miller, the guest speaker from the Sheriff's Department. She pushed away from the library doors but fell on her knees again in the blood on the hallway floor. Then she scrambled up to her feet and bolted for the main entrance. He followed, not far behind her. They heard the tire iron clatter to the floor as they escaped into the open air, the main doors closing behind them.

They were in front of the building in the open sunlight. To their right, the paved walkway sloped downward and wound around the parking lot. Beyond the path was a small, sloping field of mown grass that ended at a line of trees not far away. They bolted down the walkway, across the field, and into the line of dense trees.

They ran through the brush and between the trees for a long time, far out of sight of the school building, until they came to something of a clearing. There they stopped. Dr. Miller fell to his knees, gasping for breath.

Cathy stopped in the middle of the clearing. She bent down with her hands on her knees and breathed in the clean air. Then she straightened and stood upright, and tipped her head back, throwing her face into the sun. After the cold and bloody hall, the sun seemed so bright and warm that it was as though she had never truly known it. She wanted to run upwards to the sun, to embrace it, to kiss its warmth forever.

"We can't stay here for too long," panted Dr. Miller. "We'll have to keep moving soon. Just—I need to catch my breath."

He fell back against a tree trunk and tipped his head back, his eyes closed, and his face twisted in a grimace from exertion.

"Who are they?" she asked.

"I'm not sure," he panted.

"Can I stay with you?"

He wiped the sweat off of his brow with his sleeve. He opened one eye, squinting at the sun. "Sure," he said. "I don't know how much good I'll be to ya."

"I'll be safer with you than I will be on my own."

He looked at her from his squinting eye, nodded slightly, and then closed his eye again.

"Your chances for survival go up from zero percent to one percent." He panted heavily and licked his lips.

Cathy looked around the forest. They seemed to be safe.

"What do they want?" she said. "Why are they—attacking like that?"

He took a deep breath and exhaled slowly, deliberately. Then he said, "Lady, I know as much as you do." He was breathing a little easier now. "They seem to be going after brains. They eat the brains. They eat the skin too, the flesh—but it seems like the brain is mostly what they're after."

"But why?"

"Goddamn it, I don't know," he said abruptly. "I'm just telling you what I've seen. Yeah, I'll tell you what I've seen, so maybe you'll have a better chance at defending yourself." He opened the eye again and squinted at her. "They attack together, but not really in a pack, like, it's not organized. They go after the brain. I saw someone escape an attack, but they had been bitten. The bite was infected or something, and it all happened really fast, but before long, he had just turned into one of them."

He grimaced, gritting his teeth and closing his eyes.

"I was in the office," he said. "We could see the construction workers coming toward us. The secretary, she got up and went out to see what was going on—it looked like they wanted something. Then they attacked her, and they broke the windows to the school. I was still confused, but the principal got on the intercom... thank God he was able to think faster than I was. Obviously, it did some good. You got out of it."

"It wasn't really because of the announcement..."

"We got out through the fire escape in the back. The principal, he's all right, he got in his car and went to town." Dr. Miller pulled out his cellphone from a holster on his hip, opposite the one for his gun. "Hmm, no signal. That's weird. I guess we're out of range down here. Well, I was expecting a call from him—I guess that explains why I haven't gotten it yet." He put his cellphone back. "I went back in to see if anyone else had made it. Really, I was mostly looking for my daughter, Brooke. I don't know if you know her."

"I think I had her as a freshman."

"Anyway... we need to get going..." Dr. Miller tried to lift himself up. He gasped through his teeth in pain and gave up, sliding back down along the tree trunk.

"Do you need help?" asked Cathy.

"No, I'm just—" He tried again, with the same result. He began unbuttoning his shirt from the top. "There's something in my back, or... would you mind taking a look? I think maybe something got jammed in there."

He pulled the collar of his shirt down around his shoulder, revealing the top of his neck and back. She leaned down a little. There was a dark wound just where his neck met his shoulder, so he had clearly sustained some sort of injury. She bent lower to get a closer look at it.

"Yes," she said, " I see something."

Nearer to it, she saw that it was oval-shaped. There was swelling around its edges. The skin had been torn away. The outline was jagged, like the marks of teeth—

"You got bitten," she muttered.

Dr. Miller's heavy panting stopped for a moment, and then continued, as though he had needed to hold his breath in order to take this in.

"Shit," he spat. "Goddamn it."

"It doesn't look like it's spread very far," she said. "Maybe, if you have a knife, we could cut around it..."

Dr. Miller wrinkled his face in almost a sneer at the idea. "It's too late," he said morosely.

"Can't we do something about it?"

Dr. Miller said nothing but reached down to his belt. He undid the snap on a small compartment made out of leather.

Cathy said, "How do you know how it works? What if it spreads through the skin, or something?"

Dr. Miller extracted a small white, red, and blue box and placed it on his lap. Then he reached around behind him towards another place on the belt.

"We're not far from the road. We can go and wait by the road, and maybe someone will drive by..."

Dr. Miller pulled his pistol out from behind his back and laid it in his lap next to the box. He opened the box, revealing the butts of a dozen bullets.

"They could take us to the hospital, and there, you could..."

Dr. Miller snapped the magazine from the handle, and began putting the bullets in, one by one.

"But I suppose, you're probably too weak to walk…"

"Listen, lady, I don't know if you've ever shot a gun before, but I want you to do me a favor." He snapped the magazine back into the handle. He pulled back the slide, and then snapped it back in place. He switched off the safety, and then turned the gun, holding it by the muzzle so that he held the handle out toward her.

"Here."

She took the gun from him and held it in her right hand, the weight of it pulling at her arm.

"I want you to do me the favor of giving me a death with dignity." He placed his hands in his lap like a child. "Aim it at my temple so that it goes straight through. That way you'll get my brain—I won't become one of them. Just one shot."

"But, I can't just kill you…"

"I'm dead already."

"You don't know that… We could still…"

"Just hurry up and do it already. I don't know how much longer I have."

She stared at the gun in her hand. She looked carefully at Dr. Miller's temple, which stared at her, broad and bald, like a clean piece of paper.

"Do it," he said.

Her hand shook. "No," she muttered. "I couldn't do that."

"Don't make me do it myself!" he shouted. "There isn't any honor in suicide. And besides, I might miss! You're the only way."

"No," she said again, quietly. She dropped the gun on the forest floor.

Dr. Miller looked down at the gun. "I'm trying to protect you!" he said.

He picked up the gun and thrust it out at her again by the muzzle, his hand shaking. "You don't have a lot of time left. I'm not going to do it, so you'd better hurry up and do it unless you want me to die and come back as one of those rotting corpses hungry for your—"

Cathy grasped the gun and held it up, locking her elbows and pointing it at him. Her hands trembled violently.

"Do it! Hurry up, do it!"

She fired. The gun almost jumped out of her hands. Dr. Miller uttered a weak cry. She lowered the gun and refocused her vision, and saw that she had hit him in the chest.

"Goddamn it, you couldn't even—get that right—"

She stumbled closer to him, dropping her foot, and fired the gun full in his face, fired it twice, and a third time.

When she stepped back, she dropped the gun. His face was destroyed. Pieces of bone, flesh, and brain matter had become embedded into the tree bark and spattered the ground surrounding his body. What was left of the head was bent very far back, like a gaping mouth that had overtaken the entire face in mocking laughter.

She collapsed to her knees on the ground, kneeling by the gun and the headless body. She sat there for a long while, and then she dropped her head to the ground, next to the gun, and drew her elbows in under her body against her knees and curled up her ugly hands underneath her chest. She breathed in the smell of the indifferent forest floor, and listened to the sounds of the birds singing, and the wind rustling in the trees.

***

She must have fallen asleep, for when she sat up again, her eyes had the feel of having been closed for a long time, and the sun's light shown more gently at an angle through the foliage.

The gun was still there, and the body, and the box of bullets. A name flashed through her mind: *Brooke Miller.*

She picked up the box of bullets and the gun. She couldn't remember how Dr. Miller had ejected the magazine. She fiddled around with the gun for a while, making sure that the safety switch—which she *did* remember—was engaged as she did so. At last, she released the magazine and pulled it out.

She had fired four shots. There were six bullets left in the magazine, and six in the box. She took four of the bullets from the box and loaded them into the magazine, reloaded the magazine into the handle, and took the other two bullets and put them in her pocket.

Then she rose slowly to her feet. Her legs were weak, her feet numb and heavy, and the skin of her legs was tingling. She wiped her brow with the back of the wrist of the hand that held the gun. Her forehead was more greasy than sweaty, and wiping it did little more than spread the grease around.

She felt as though she should not leave the corpse behind, but she also felt that she must do some good—that she must go back and find Brooke Miller, if she could, in honor of Dr. Miller's legacy. She felt ill prepared for this mission, of course, but she was armed with a weapon now, and at least some working knowledge of these—things.

With a certain amount of regret, she turned away from the corpse and retraced their path through the forest. Before long, she made out the structure of the school from between the trees, and at length she emerged from the woods onto the grass field.

The building stood tall and blank, indifferent and unchanged. There were no signs of anything within or without.

Judging that her passage would be clear and that she was not being observed, she headed up the hill to the main entrance of the school.

Away from the hushed ambient noises of the woods, the school grounds were strangely quiet. Her own footsteps seemed very loud, and she thought that if any of them were around, they certainly would hear and begin their pursuit. But none must have heard, for none came running.

When she reached the main entrance of the school, she stopped and looked in through the dark windows. The main entrance to the main office, and at a right turn was the hallway leading to the gymnasium and the auditorium. All was dark, and there was no motion.

She tried the door. It was still unlocked.

She pulled at it gently, trying to make as little noise as possible, and to avoid any sudden movements that might attract attention. The door opened smoothly on its hinges, making no noise, and she slipped in, ducking down out of the main line of sight from the office windows.

She looked to the left and the right of the hallway and saw that they were empty. As at the opposite end of the school, blood covered the floor in a slick layer about an inch thick. As the door closed, darkening the hallway once more, she crept deeper in. It was familiar, and she felt sick. She tightened her grip on the handle of the gun. With her left hand, she turned off the safety. Then, with more force than she imagined she would need, she pulled back the slide as she had seen Dr. Miller do.

She crept across the empty hall toward the office with some vague idea that starting at the central location of the school would give her a better idea of whether or not Brooke Miller was alive or not. Deep down, she knew this to be absurd, but no better solution presented itself.

Once she had crossed the hall, she pried open the office door, slowly and quietly, and still staying low. She slid inside and let the door close behind her. It latched shut with a click. The office was dark and silent. She stood and walked into the room.

Before she could react, one was upon her—she felt its cold fingers on the back of her arm and its pressure on her—she spun and fell back, trembling. It loomed over her and she looked up at the nearly glowing eyes in the darkness. Another stood behind it and a third above her from the opposite direction. She flailed wildly, knocking one down, but the other two clutched at her with a force so strong that they tore her skin as she scrambled to get away.

With great difficulty, she brought herself to her feet, and looking up she saw that there were a great many of them gathered there in the office—fifteen, maybe more.

She looked at them desperately through the darkness, trying to make out their features. The hideous transformation that they had undergone made many of them anonymous and unrecognizable. She did not recognize Brooke Miller, but even if Brooke was among them, it would not have mattered. If Brooke were alive and unchanged, somewhere else in the building, that would not have mattered either. She was up against too great a number.

Then among the pairs of eyes were two that caught her attention—two that she recognized. They were hollow and indifferent, but they were set in a face that, despite its terrifyingly mangled and disfigured aspect, told of grief so profound that it had written itself across the face in permanence that transgressed both death and unnatural resurrection. They were Sara's.

At this sight, terror of a different sort struck at Cathy and with what little strength and courage she could muster at the instant, she threw herself into the creatures behind her and ran for the workroom, the entrance to which lay at the back of the office behind the secretary's desk. She hurled herself through the doorway and slammed the door shut on the horde, throwing it shut with her entire body. Then, amidst the pounding of their hands, and the screeches and howls of their hungry incantations, she slid down the door onto her knees beside it.

She looked at the gun, turning it over in her hands the dark. Then she noticed something on her hand—a dark spot on the back of it near the base of her left thumb. A bite.

Something inside her sank with a force that seemed to tear through her, a feeling so profound that it was as though some physical membrane or barrier inside of her had just been broken. The physicality of it suggested at first that it was the result of having been bitten, but the feeling had occurred at the sight of the thing—not as a result of the thing itself.

Then she felt a deep despair. It was more than just despair that arose from her hopeless situation—it had merely unlocked this despair *from within*, which transcended it. It was as though she had always carried the despair with her, and it had been kept secret from her until this very moment.

Then she remembered the stillborn infant, an image that returned in her psyche as though it were the only image she had ever really seen in her life: a blue stillborn infant with its purple cord around its neck. She wished to return to the infant, to pick it up and hold it as though that would bring it back to life—not some insensate mockery of life, but *real* life—even though she knew this to be impossible.

But there was something beneath her despair, something that except for the despair she never would have known was there either—like a quiet noise that she never would have heard unless it were in the midst of a deathlike silence. This thing beneath the despair found its expression in something like anger, but without rage, or determination, but without a goal.

All that she had known had fallen away from her, and what remained, or what now presented itself, was utterly foreign. There was nothing sensible to it, so it was not with any sense that she rose from her crouched position on the floor and went to the worktable. She knew that what she would do would be painful and would likely fail. But for the first time, success and failure seemed altogether irrelevant. Something had been upheaved inside of her. A profound shift had taken place.

She set the gun on the counter and took hold of the paper cutter with her thin, wiry, ugly hand. Holding it down, she wrenched the metal paper guide from the wooden base and lay it aside. Then she positioned her left arm on the base so that her other thin, wiry, ugly hand, the hand that had been bitten, hung over the edge, the joint of her wrist resting on the metal corner. She loosened the joint, hoping to allow for an easier passage of the blade. She tried the path of the blade and let it touch the skin of her wrist gently as confirmation that her blow would hit its mark. Her arm lay heavily on the wood.

Then she swung with a force so strong that it was as though God himself had driven down the blade.

The bones cracked at the impact and a spray of warm blood erupted in her face. A shock—not of pain, but of a galvanizing, almost electric sensation—coursed through her arm and seemed to engulf her entire body for a moment. She blinked away the blood and looked down. It had come free, clean and easy, as though it had always been meant to come off.

She sat down and reached her right hand up to the sleeve of her left arm and tugged on it as hard as she could. The fabric was flimsy and ripped free easily. She balled it up into a large, loose wad, and pressed it against the bleeding stump of her left wrist. She rose and stood at the worktable again, and this time, took a rubber band from a tray and wrapped the band around the torn blouse sleeve, blotting the wound and also acting as a makeshift tourniquet.

The blade's attachment had weakened with the strike, and it lay askew against the base. She pulled at the handle on the blade and twisted it. It came free of the bolt and came off in her hand.

She decided to leave the gun. She wasn't able to reload it anymore. And the blade needed no reloading.

The door thudded and the creatures moaned from without.

She pressed the blade flat against her face and closed her eyes.

Then, after a moment, she opened them again and looked at the door.

She knew that Sara was outside. She knew that she would have to face her at least once more. But she knew that it was not really Sara. It was some corruption of the flesh, a deception of biology, or nature, or—she didn't know what—but it was not really Sara. She was certain of that.

Holding the blade steadily and firmly in hand, she lifted her leg and placed her heel on the handle of the door. The latch clicked, and the door swung open.

THEY RETURN

Loneliness had become a part of him. Loneliness was his dark and tattooed skin; it felt the vacant air and rose in ridges at the cold. It was the sight of his eyes; it made clear the emptiness of the house, the hills, the sky. It heard all that he heard, muffled with the cotton of the dead silence of the day.

It went with him at night when they came out of the darkness, when they visited him one after another. It overcame him and rendered him powerless as he stared at the distorted faces of his past, driving them back into the woods, firing shot after useless shot into their impossible bodies. And when he returned to the house at dawn, spent after the nightly cycle of warfare, Loneliness took him in her ambivalent arms and laid him down on the cot and watched disdainfully as he fought against the heresy of daylight for sleep.

He would wake in the evening, and before going out into the dark with his gun, he would refill the generator with gasoline, prepare food on the stove and eat it, and perform various maintenance tasks about the house. At dusk, he would open his Bible and read it in preparation for the work of the night. This drove Loneliness back a little.

He knew that God was watching over him. But he had felt it more keenly when he was the only one, when Loneliness had been only a vague figure looming on the horizon of every moment. But now she stood in every doorway of every room, watching without eyes, speaking without words, crawling through the skin over his skull. The emptiness and silence of the house seemed to suggest to him her indifference to his existence and it had all but drowned out any real sense he had of God.

As he often did, he looked down at his tattooed arm to remind himself of his own name—"JUDE"—and he reminded himself of his name to confirm his own existence. He closed the Bible on the desk and looked up at the faux-gold cross which he had hung on the wall. It had been in the house when he had arrived. He had hung it very high, far up the wall, so that he could see it from every room of the house. Incidentally, it looked better far away than up close; there was some bezeling on it that disagreed with his taste and made the cross seem old-fashioned and womanish.

He set his teeth and rose from the desk. His body imbued with Loneliness, he plunged into the twilight and racked the slide on his pistol. The metallic *click-click* burst through the silence and died in the distant brush.

He waited in the thickening dark. The sound of the vacant wind tore through the trees at the edge of the field and whispered through the grass as it blew nearer to him.

He had been fighting a cold recently, and without thinking, he inhaled through his nose violently, snapping back the mucus.

The brush stirred, and when he heard the leaves rustle, he realized his mistake.

Then, as they had done before, and as he knew they would, they came out of the trees at the far end of the field. He shuddered. He gripped the pistol tightly. He waited until they were in range.

Gradually, their pace increased until they were running. Their arms hung awkwardly to the sides as though numb and immobile although their legs moved very quickly. Under different circumstances, he might have found it comical.

When they were in range, he opened fire. The pistol shot rang out into the night. The impact of the bullet tore at the shoulder of one, slowing it down so that the pack overtook it. He shot again. This time, he hit one full in the chest. The impact drove it backward into the crowd, but then the crowd pushed it forward again and trampled it.

Now they were close enough that he could make out their faces. Tonight, as every night, he expected the faces to be rotting or decayed like some of the others, or to retain the disfiguring injuries they had sustained from the nights previous when he had fought them off before. But no—always to his horror, the faces remained unchanged, and virtually as they had been in life.

There in the crowd was Treyvon Marsh. In a previous life, Treyvon had been a drug dealer from a gang that was rival to Jude's. He had shot him to death during a skirmish. Treyvon had been nineteen at the time, although he had already built up for himself a reputation among the gangs for his wild, reckless fighting style. Jude had been on higher alert than normal, and when he saw Treyvon, he had not hesitated. In death, Treyvon had seemed so much like a child, and Jude had wondered if the reputation weren't some wild fabrication, or if he had killed the wrong person altogether. In any case, he had been able to claim self-defense. Treyvon had become another gangland statistic, and Jude had gone free, only mildly molested by the police, and unprosecuted.

Treyvon, now returned, seemed all the more grotesque for his childlike features. The large lips and poorly proportioned nose stood out on his face in a rotten mockery of childishness, and he, like all the rest, was driven with a singular ravenous intent devoid of innocence.

There was Michael Harris, who had embezzled and lied to the boss about his take; Jude had carried out the hit. He had been an older man, middle-aged, white. Jude had made it look like an accident. He had lured him to a remote location with a blackmail threat. Although Jude had not expected him to, Harris had actually brought money with him, hoping to pay off his blackmailer. Jude disposed of him from a height, making sure that it would seem that he had tripped and fallen; and he had kept the money for himself.

Now Harris was back, more pale than ever, his eyes red-rimmed, his mouth black. His body was still bent from the fall he had taken, but it did not impede him any; he ran as fast as the others, if not faster, and sought for Jude with the same ravenous zeal driving the horde.

There was Arionna Willis, the prostitute who had gotten shot in the crossfire during a deal gone wrong; he had held her as she bled out and died. This was one of the most painful of all his memories. When he had met her, he had felt at first a vague uneasiness and then eventually a burning and profound disquiet. He was certain that she was good, and yet she was doing bad things, involved with bad people. And as he grew to know her better and became more convinced of this, he had begun to reflect upon himself and see himself in the same light. He had been good; how had he gone so wrong? But before this notion had had time to fully materialize in him, they had found themselves in the midst of the fallout of a betrayal, facing down several armed thugs at once. A bullet that had been meant for him had found her.

After her death, he had continued with the thug life, although with an unshakable sense of disquiet. Eventually, he had been charged and convicted for dealing, and gone to prison. In prison, he had met with a pastor ministering there and been converted to Christianity. He had repented and confessed of all these and other sins and had been washed clean. He had put his former life behind him and had moved forward as a changed man. But the faces and the bodies had all returned, and they were coming for him again tonight.

She, too, had come back, a horrible monstrosity, awful in her marred beauty, and hideous in her inhuman intent. He could barely stand to look at her, let alone defend himself from her attacks—but he went through with it, night after night, against her and all the others.

A clammy chill descended on his body. It was not merely the familiar rush of adrenaline he felt before a fight, but also a constricted feeling in his throat and tingling in his forehead and around his ears. These faces, these terrible reminders of his former life, unnaturally living memories—why had they sought him out after they had returned? Why did they *continue* to seek him out? How had they found him out here in the country, far from the city of that former life and its past sins? Even more strange was that some of the dead he had never been involved with directly; he had not been responsible for their deaths. But sometimes these were even more terrifying than his own victims when they appeared. And why, after countless nights of defending himself and his house from them, maiming them, destroying them—did they return again and again, seemingly stronger than before?

Defense had become as routine to him as clipping his fingernails. As soon as several had fallen from bullets and he had judged the crowd thin enough to manage, he dropped the pistol and drew his machete. They rushed him; he swung powerfully. The machete struck flesh and bone and tore through with great force. Black, vile blood spurted onto his arms and face. He pulled back but the machete pulled at his wrist. It had gotten lodged in a bone; the blade was getting dull. After he had pulled it free, he swung again into the crowd, back and forth, rapidly and haphazardly. The crowd was so thick around him that careful aim was not necessary; every stroke cut deep through the rank flesh. He ducked below the cold fingers that reached for his face and eyes. He thrust forward with the blade and threw his weight into the forward motion. What remained of the crowd toppled over. He rolled to the side, and then got back on his feet and stood over the pile. He raised the machete, and held.

He looked down. On the top of the pile was Treyvon Marsh. He looked into Treyvon's eyes, which were looking back up at his own from the side, their faces perpendicular. The eyes looked at him with a vacant gaze that seemed almost contemptuous. The mouth opened as though it were going to say something but instead vomited up a gush of black blood.

He struck down with the machete quickly and decisively and clove the face in two lengthwise across the mouth. Black liquid shot upward in fat droplets and the blade cracked against the teeth. The jawbone dislocated and the cheeks split as if in mocking, silent laughter. The rows of teeth appeared small in the now gaping mouth, like a mule when it brays. The eyes, pushed slightly out of the soft sockets by the pressure of the blow, lolled crazily to either side.

The cadaver lay limp and still, yet its mocking, wild-eyed, ass-like gaze tormented Jude. There was no ridding himself of the chill it instilled. Time became recursive and meaningless.

But there were still others. He lifted the machete from the chopped face and swung rapidly at the advancing crowd. He backed away as he swung, going for the door. He had done this so many times before that he did not need to look behind him.

Then, turning around with a final swing, he drew the blade across the horde in an arc that met three of their throats at once. The jaws and heads dropped as black blood gushed from the wounds, and the bodies fell. In the house at last, he slammed the door on the advancing throng, closing them out. Cold, clammy hands clapped at the door and wall. He fell to the floor and clasped the machete, sticky with black blood, to his chest. He closed his eyes tightly and his body shook as the images of the faces raced through his mind, and the pounding on the walls reverberated through his head.

"God, God…" he pleaded. "What can I do? What can I do?"

***

He woke with a start and shivered. He sat with his back still to the door and the cold machete in his hand. The house had lost heat in the night. He was still drenched in sweat, shivering with a chill. The blood had dried on the machete. He stood up suddenly and the machete fell, the blood flaking off in dry, dark-brown chunks.

He went to the window. An angry-looking dawn had set a dormant glow alight in a distant corner of the horizon, like an orange and red wound on the still deep-blue sky.

He opened the door and went out. The morning was fresh; the day would be hot.

He went around to the side of the house where there were doors to a storm cellar. The weathered white doors were closed and locked with a padlock. He stooped down beside them and put out his hand. He stuck his finger in the padlock and tugged at it; the lock held tight. He reached into his pocket and took out the key, which was on a large ring to prevent it from getting lost. He unlocked the padlock and threw the doors open. Inside was a large stockpile of supplies; cans of food, jugs of gas, boxes of bullets, and more.

He heaved a sigh of relief, as though in the cellar he kept his heart itself.

He shut the doors slowly, with an air of sober gratitude, and closed the heavy padlock. He was always very careful to keep the door closed and locked, and it gave him a measure of satisfaction merely to do so.

He bowed his head and closed his eyes. Leaning over the closed and locked doors of the cellar, he said a prayer of thanks to God that he had been able to keep his supplies safe.

The Lord is my shepherd; I shall not want...

He returned to the dead silent house, his limbs feeling weak. He collapsed onto his cot in the bedroom and fell fast asleep.

***

He awoke suddenly. He thought that it had been a noise that had awakened him, but in the half-memory of his emergent consciousness still enveloped by a haze of sleep, he could not be sure that he had heard anything at all. He sat up in his cot. His room was dark; he had boarded up the windows some time ago, and light never entered. He did not know if it was night or day, or how long he had slept. He strained his ears, listening for whatever sound had awakened him in case it repeated itself.

The silence grew to a harsh ring that throttled his ears; the emptiness became a fullness like Loneliness herself who filled all the empty spaces of his house and of his life.

Then the silence was shattered by a soft but definite rustle of the brush that sounded as though it were just on the other side of his bedroom wall. He stiffened and then forced himself to rise, making as little noise as possible. Slowly and cautiously, he reached his hand out for the doorknob and opened his bedroom door.

It was daylight. The sun crept stealthily into the house through the gaps in the boarded-up windows with an indeterminate yellow glow.

So it was not them. But he had heard the noise just the same. An animal? Something attracted by the scent of something in the supply shed?

He took up his pistol from the desk where his Bible lay, snapped a magazine into the handle, and racked the slide. The gun ready in his right hand, he opened the front door with his left and stepped out into the morning glow.

It was mid-morning, and the air was not yet hot. It was fresh and cooling, and it energized Jude despite his fatigue. The yellow sun bathed the field in a pleasant, even light, although he could not see the sun itself. In the distance, the trees stood dark against the brightening sky. A light breeze rustled the brush and the gold-green grass; other than that, it was quiet.

At the side of the house were two figures dressed in rags. The daylight did not seem to become them. The first was a woman, probably middle-aged, although she was so dirty and her rags were so unbecoming that she seemed an old hag. The other was a boy, about ten by Jude's estimation, covered in the same dirt. But the boy had clear blue eyes that peeped out from under a mess of shaggy hair and that, rather than merely reflecting the light of the sun, seemed to share its illumination.

The two started at the sight of Jude's large frame and at the gun pointed at them. They must have seen the house and probably assumed it to be uninhabited, as he had when he had first arrived. He lowered the gun.

For a long time, no one said anything. The kind thing to do would be to invite them in and give them something to eat or drink; but he had spent a long time building up his own resources and was loath to simply give them away. They, on the other hand, were probably intimidated and unsure of his intentions; even though it was no longer pointed at them, the gun was still held by him.

At last, he muttered, "Well, come inside—quickly."

They scurried along the side of the house, clinging to it as though it would protect them on the outside as well as in, and slid in at the door as though compelled by gravity. He closed the door behind them. He watched them and kept his gun gripped firmly in his large hand.

In the main room, they stood close together, looking about the house. It was dirty, but livable; it invited living. The furniture that had come with the house had been pushed back against the rear door that no longer latched shut or locked. In the past, the rear door had opened out to a deck, but the deck now no longer existed; Jude had long ago chopped it into firewood. An old rug covered most of the main area and was thick with dust. The house had a musty smell and an insurgent patch of angry-looking mold was festering beneath the peeling paper of a wall that had suffered water damage. Still, the kitchen was functional and over the dank baseline mustiness floated the savory smell of frequent cooking— of grease and fried hash and seasoned iron. The light of the sun creeping through the air in thin bands from between the gaps in the boards seemed to catch itself up in the haze of the air. The light hinted at something long-forgotten—of easy summer days, of rest, perhaps even of joy.

The two abject figures exhibited an apparent relief by the dropping of their hunched shoulders. They still remained silent. The woman's head was bowed, and she did not make eye contact with the man. Her gesture seemed to convey a sense of humility and gratitude, and yet something else about her still implored him for something more.

After a long silence, he anticipated the request she might have intended him to infer and said, "You can't stay here. I don't got enough room for you."

The woman's eyes fell to the floor which was empty except for the large, bare, dusty rug. Then suddenly she looked back up at him and darted her eyes about the room.

"Are you here alone?"

"Yes, it's just me," he said. He folded his arms across his chest, thick and muscular.

"We need help," the woman said at last, her voice weakened with the fatigue of travel and hunger but with a firmness and dignity that cut through.

"There's just not enough to go around. You know—you could sleep on the floor or something, but... then what? See, that's what I'm always thinking. What happens then? I'm just going to have to kick you out sooner or later. I'm always thinking what happens down the road, what's gonna happen a long time from now. Most people, they just think about tomorrow. Or maybe even just tonight. But I'm trying to think bigger than that."

The woman tried to conceal the fact that she felt impugned by what he had said but failed. "Tomorrow is important too. So is tonight."

"But that can't be just all we think, you know? Yeah, yeah, tonight is important, and we have to plan for tomorrow. But the tomorrows just go on forever if you ain't thinking about the last tomorrow."

Her face now evinced disgust. "The 'last' tomorrow."

Jude had already been feeling defensive, and now he drew his arms tighter across his chest as he inhaled, drew his head back, and looked down at her seriously.

"You think this will ever end?" she said.

"Yes."

She nearly scoffed at him. "This will never end. All we have are a bunch of tomorrows—tomorrow, and tomorrow's tomorrow...and nothing else. There is no 'end,' except, maybe, when we die." She sighed and her shoulders dropped. "And that's not even an end anymore."

"That's not all," he said.

Her disgust morphed into contempt. "So you're one of those who's still holding on to hope, eh? One of the *hopeful* ones."

Jude steeled himself with willpower. He searched deep inside himself for the strong iron surety to which he always clung. He reframed his argument.

"I can't keep you safe here. That's the honest truth. They come at night mostly, and sometimes during the day. Sometimes they stay away so long I think they're gone altogether, that I got rid of 'em. But then they come back. I can't predict it, but they come back. You see—I kill 'em, but it doesn't matter. I even chop 'em up and stuff—I do whatever I want, but it makes no difference. It's like nothing ever happened to 'em." He lowered his voice intensely, letting her in on a secret that he wasn't quite sure she would believe. "They followed me here. Used to be I could just blow their brains out. But now I can do any damn thing to 'em I can think of, and they—they just come back! I think… I think I must be going nuts. I wish I knew how to make it stop!"

His voice had intensified feverishly and the woman looked frightened—of what he didn't know; of them, or of him, or perhaps both.

The whole time, the boy had been staring intently at him. The boy's features were disproportionate as is common to boys in the middle stage of their maturation. His ears were large and flat on top, and his nose had grown too big for the rest of his face, all of which gave him the semblance of a lamb. There was something familiar to Jude about his eyes, but also something completely alien at the same time. His eyes suggested the potentiality of some sort of intimate connection while being at the same time totally unreadable and unknowable.

Then, in a wave of acute awareness, Jude realized that the boy and the woman were unrelated. The boy seemed oddly aloof to her, and she to him; although they stood close to each other, no bond existed between them. They were probably strangers who had met through circumstance and had ended up traveling together out of necessity.

He felt a connection to the boy, however. The boy's eye had an almost fanatical gleam.

"How old is the boy?" he asked.

"I don't know," the woman said. "He won't speak to me."

"You been together long?"

"Not long. But I suppose long enough. He seems timid maybe."

Jude looked long and hard at the boy. The boy stared back at him with an incongruous face—the eyes of a lion in the face of a lamb.

"He's got a spark in his eye," Jude said at length. "He's a little hellion." Just beneath the surface of his face, a smile loomed.

"He's no hellion," the woman said. "I think he's a good boy. He's stayed by me the whole time, and he hasn't given me any trouble. And look at him. He's just a sweet boy. Poor thing has probably lost his parents, or been abandoned by them. He probably can't speak for the grief of losing them."

"He may be a sweet boy now, but you just let him live a little longer, and you'll see." He gave an upward thrust of his head. "Every boy got a little hellion in him. If you want to let him grow up to be a man, you gotta recognize that. You gotta let him let it out a little."

The woman looked at him coolly. He could sense her becoming defensive of the boy. Her defensiveness surprised him. The boy had only been with her a short time and had not even spoken to her.

"You don't know him," he said. "You don't know what it is to be a man."

Suddenly, he was very tired. He realized that he had not sat for a long time. The night of fighting and little sleep had made him weary, and the adrenaline of first meeting them had worn off. The stress was now exacting a different cost from him.

The defensive look on the woman's face dissipated, and in its place arose a plastic-like mask of apathy. She said, "Well, he's just a burden to me. If you want to keep him and raise him up 'to be a man,' you're welcome to him. I can see you don't want to help *me*, so I'll be on my way." She turned to leave.

"Now wait a minute," he said, catching her arm.

He was unsure if her movement was a bluff, but by the time the doubt of its genuineness had sprung to his mind, it was too late; he had already acted. He was unsure also whether it was her apathy or her attachment to the boy that was the more genuine. But her statement had cut him, and he held her arm in a strong grip.

"You can stay if you want, I suppose—as long as you know that they come here often, and at random… and that there's nothing I can do about them. There's nothing I can do to keep you safe. Do you understand that?"

"Don't keep me out of pity," she said, not trying to wrench herself free of his grip but not succumbing to it either. "I don't want your pity."

"Stay," he said firmly. "We're all in this together. I was—I was wrong to—I was wrong not to offer to have you stay. But mind you—don't try anything funny. We're all in this together, but to some people, that means that we're none of us in it together, and we're all only in it by ourselves. Now I'm not pitying you. I don't pity anyone. You can pity yourself. But stay. I want you to stay."

Slowly, she acquiesced and rotated her body back toward him, reneging to some extent her previous motion. He let go of her arm and then took a step backward in response to the newly established joint tenancy of the room in which they stood. The woman and the boy looked about the room with wandering eyes as though, now that they were officially welcome to inhabit the room, their cognition of it had been altered or increased. It echoed the looks they had given the room at their first entrance, and for some reason, this repetition troubled Jude greatly. Not seeing anywhere to sit with their roving eyes, the woman and the boy simply walked into the middle of the room, to the center of the rug, and stood there without resolution.

Jude wanted to invite them to sit, but the furniture pushed up against the rear entrance did not seem a particularly hospitable proposition, and the hard floor even less inviting. He waved his hand at them and said, "Well, make yourselves at home."

The woman and the boy did not move.

The man's stomach suddenly clenched with hunger, and at this, he realized that the boy and the women were probably also hungry. He thought, with a pang of regret, of the storage shed outside. But he had committed himself to the unmanly task of hospitality, and the shed was where the food was.

"Boy, what's your name?" he said.

The boy did not answer.

"Do you know his name?" he asked.

"No," said the woman.

"Well, kid, follow me," he said. "Let's get us something to eat."

The boy obligingly left the side of the woman and fell in step beside him as he led the way out of the house.

The sunlight was warm and inviting, and with the boy beside him, it was hard for Jude to remember that even at this time of day the others might appear. It had not been for a long time that they had amassed and attacked in the kind of broad daylight in which they stood right now, but it remained a distinct possibility. He had to remind himself to scan the surroundings for signs of movement. Ironically, the glare of the sunlight made it harder for him to discern what lay at the edge of the dark trees in the distance; the brilliance of the sun and the clear-blue sky reflected off of the field in a stunning green glare that made it seem as though the tree line were farther away from the house than it was. Or maybe the distance that he now gauged was the true one, and it was only the distortion of the thick night that had made him think it was closer than he perceived it to be now.

At the back of the house lay the white doors to the storm cellar. The sunlight played at it as though it wished to bleach it white again, but the stubborn paint reacted by wrinkling and peeling, exposing more of the grey wood underneath. Jude approached it hastily as though he were anxious to confirm its existence by his touch. He laid his hands on it. The paint was faintly warm from the heat of the sun, about the temperature of his own body.

He drew the key out of his jeans pocket and held it out toward the lock as though it were a wild animal; he treated it gently so as not to tempt it into some wild, unpredictable action. As he was turning the key in the lock, he noticed the boy looking at his tattooed arms.

"My name is Jude," he said to the boy. "I had it tattooed on my arm when I changed it. Yes, I changed my name. It used to be Tyrone. That was in a previous life."

The lock clicked and popped open. He was regretful, for a moment, for having let the boy see him open the lock, although the location of the lock and how it worked was no great secret, and the boy seemed to present no threat. For Jude, the opening of the shed had become a private, intimate activity and instinctively he felt defensive. He looked at the boy's lamb-like face and eyes full of sparks, and perceived both the familiarity and the incomprehensibility that he had noted earlier. He told himself against his initial and probably more sensible instinct that it was safe for the boy to witness the process of the unlocking of the shed. He was also curious to hear some words from the boy; he imagined hopefully that the boy would recognize the intimacy of the opening of the shed, and that it would encourage him to speak. So he opened it. Daylight poured in, cascading onto the stacks of cans and towers of boxes.

"This is what I've been living off of," he said. "It's a secret, you understand? You don't tell anybody about it, do you hear?"

He searched the boy for a sign of agreement, or even of understanding, but there was none. The boy only stared at him intently.

"That old bitch in there don't understand. She ain't been where I been. She wouldn't understand. Don't tell her what's in here, you understand?"

Again, there was no look of understanding, but only the sparks that seemed to fly from the boy's eyes into and through him.

He stepped into the shed. Inside, it was cool and dark, an agreeable contrast to the still heat of the sun against the side of the house. The boy made a motion to follow him in, but Jude held out his hand and said, "No. You stay outside." He opened up a box and removed some of its contents and then filled it back up with other various cans. As he rummaged through the goods in the shed, he said to the boy:

"When I was kid, I got busted for dropping bricks off a bridge over the freeway. One of the bricks went straight into a window; the driver freaked, swerved, rolled over, and collided with a truck. The driver died. I didn't go to jail or nothing. The judge ruled that we were just being stupid kids. But my dad, *he* didn't let me forget. He would remind me every day I was a killer. He would hit me over the head and shove me around. He didn't treat me like my brothers and sisters. He did it even when I got older and it got so I couldn't take it no more. So then I left. I joined a gang—since I was a killer anyway—and the gang became like a new family to me. They treated me with *respect*. They respected me if I earned it."

He closed up the box, came back out of the shed and handed it to the boy. "Here," he said. "You hold this." He went back in and began to do the same with another box.

"I have killed men," he went on, "not just the one off the bridge, but other men. I once killed a man with his own knife. He was trying to kill me. He came at me in an alley. Fool was clumsy. I took the knife from him and I stabbed him in the throat."

He emerged in the sunlight, his head hung down.

"I never lost a fight by myself. Even when there was more than one guy against me—three even. I killed three men by myself. With only a blade."

The boy offered no evidence of a response, if he had one. The piercing eyes seemed to indicate a further curiosity, however. They presented an insatiable thirst, yet Jude did not know what might satisfy it. They demanded, yet Jude could not interpret nor discern how to meet the demand.

At some length, Jude set his box down on the grass clumped up against the side of the house. With a routine, practiced manner, Jude tenderly closed the doors.

"I done lots of terrible things like that," Jude added quietly, muttering the words toward the closed cellar doors. "But thank God I been forgiven. That's all behind me now."

He replaced the lock over the doors. Some of the withering paint flecked off onto his hand, and he shook it off abruptly. He turned the key in the lock and, just for good measure, pulled at it to test its strength. It held fast.

"Let's go," he said.

The two of them retraced their steps around the side of the house to the door. Jude cast a half-glance over his shoulder at the shed, at the lock hanging closed on the latch just before turning the corner. He was mostly satisfied.

With the boy following him, Jude went inside the house to the kitchen with the box of food where he opened it and took out two cans of corned beef hash—one for him, and one for his guests. He turned on the gas, which he had had to connect to a tank of propane next to it since the tank connected to the exterior of the house had been drained. As the skillet heated, he opened the cans with the can opener, and then dumped their contents onto the skillet. The food crackled and sizzled on contact, and he stirred it quickly with a steel spatula.

"Someday this propane gonna run out," he said. "Then it'll just have to be eaten cold."

"What happens when you run out of *food?*" asked the woman bitterly.

Then you can fuck yourself, thought Jude, although he did not say it; it was not a Christian thing to say, and he did not want to misrepresent himself.

He switched off the gas and brought the hot skillet over, the food still sizzling. He stirred it once more, and as the sizzling subsided, he set the skillet down on a bare area of the wood floor.

"Be careful, it's hot," he said.

They ate the morsels of beef and potatoes with their fingers and did not say anything and the skillet kept the food warm until the very end. When they had finished the pieces of food, they wiped the skillet with their fingers and licked the salty fat off of them. Then they sat back, their stomachs satisfied for the moment. The boy looked at the man, and the man at the boy. The woman rose and walked about the room as though with some purpose.

She looked at the walls as had been the fashion when there were things to look at on walls where people lived, and she stopped when there was a thing to look at—the golden cross. Her expression toward it was the same plastic apathy as before.

"This yours?" she said to him in a voice so low that he wondered for a moment if he had misheard her saying something different to herself.

Jude stood and walked toward her. "It came with the house," he said, but not wanting to misrepresent himself, he added, "It was in a dresser drawer; I hung it there. The Bible is mine."

The woman sniffed—or was it a scoff?

Jude felt himself stiffening again, searching inside himself for that iron willpower on which he would have to stand as he engaged the woman.

"You don't have to agree with it," he said, his voice firm. "You just have to respect it."

More quickly than he expected, the woman retorted, "Why should I respect what is wrong? You can delude yourself if you want—I won't challenge you—but I don't have to respect you or what you do."

Jude held out his black, tattooed arms. "You see this?" he said.

She looked down at them, saying nothing, only waiting.

"This is my name. My name is Jude. I changed it when I became a Christian. My name was Tyrone, and I was a bad man. I trafficked drugs, and I killed many men." He took a step toward her, still brandishing his muscly arms. "Do you know anything about being bad, and then repenting and doing good? When you can say that you been through what I been through, then you can judge. But until then, you'd do best to keep your mouth shut."

She looked up from his arms into his face. Her brows were firmly set, demonstrating something of acquiescence, but not shame or submission.

"You best respect what you don't understand," Jude said.

The woman said nothing.

Jude continued, "You know nothing about what it means to be a man—what it takes to become one."

"You're right, I don't know anything about being a man, or what it takes to be one," said the woman. "And if you need to invent a God to help you get there, I suppose there's nothing I can say about it. But look at yourself—you call yourself a man, a grown man, and you're still hanging onto fairy tales to help you get through."

"Fairy tales…" Rage welled up within him. He felt his face flush, his ears tingle. If she had been a man, he might have punched her.

"Look around you—if there is a God, he clearly doesn't care what happens to us. How can you continue to believe after all that's happened?"

Jude fumed. He felt his will harden again, into iron, into lead.

She continued, "A real man would be able to face the facts—a real man would be able to get along on his own."

Jude suddenly gripped her arms with his thick hands. He looked sternly in her face and breathed, "But I *have* gotten along on my own, and don't you see, that's the glory of it? I believe in him and I have trusted in him, and he has provided for me. He's made me *who* I am and *what* I am… Through him, we are *more* than conquerors. Like I said, you better shut your mouth about things you don't know nothing about, if you know what's good for you."

She was unaffected and stared back into his face.

"You can't even keep us safe," she said.

He let go of her, throwing his open hands up and coughing in disgust, and he turned away from her. The sun had crossed the sky and the afternoon light shone in thin beams through the cracks in the boards, lighting and warming the stuffy air of the house. The golden cross on the wall seemed almost hidden on the far wall where he now looked.

Then he realized that the boy was not in the room.

"Where's the boy?" he asked.

"How should I know?" she asked. "He's not mine."

Jude took two quick, heavy steps across the wooden floor and opened the front door, letting in the white afternoon light.

He looked around the sides of the house, first to the right, then to the left. He did not see the boy. He walked briskly around the perimeter, rounding the corner where the cellar lay. And there was the boy—and the cellar doors open, the boy standing there looking in with the same lack of expression he had worn since his arrival.

At the sight of it, an acute shock struck Jude and overcame him. His throat constricted and his heart beat as though it would burst out of his chest.

"Boy!" Jude shouted. "Boy!"

He ran to the cellar, and pushed the boy to the ground. He threw the doors closed, and quickly fastened the metal padlock.

"What the hell were you doing? Didn't I tell you—?"

The boy had gotten up and was standing still, staring at Jude with his cold, blue eyes.

"What were you doing?" Jude demanded, his voice raised and his arm in the air.

The boy did not speak. Jude was fairly certain then that the boy could speak, but that he only refused to—that the boy was distrustful, that he was biding his time. It was as though his lack of speech *was* itself a form of speech, and it came across sinister and intimidating.

91

"Get in the house," Jude growled. He moved toward the boy, ready to physically compel him to follow the order, but the boy had already complied and was walking to the house as though nothing had happened. Jude followed him. Their feet treaded quietly on the weedy growth that surrounded the house.

Once they were both inside, Jude addressed both of them.

"Look," he said. "Look now. You two got to get out. I been here by myself because I don't trust nobody. Now, I let you in out of the goodness of my heart, I gave you food and shelter for a little bit, but now you got to get out."

"Why, what's he done?" said the woman.

"He—" Jude hesitated, but he was too upset to formulate some story other than what had actually happened. "He busted into the shed where I keep all my goods, and after I told him specifically not to do it."

"So you're driving us *both* out?"

"Look, I already told you you couldn't stay here long, and now my trust has been betrayed. You got to get out. I can't keep you here."

"You mean you don't want us here."

"Look, lady, whatever—" He sighed. "You see, as soon as there's two of us, or three of us, or more, we're a society. And a society's got to live by rules. Now *I* set down the rules, and then the rules is broken, and so there's got to be consequences. That's just how it is. A society's got to have rules, and a society's got to live by the rules—otherwise, it don't work. So I can't have you around. You got to go."

"Well," said the woman, looking down, shrugging, and taking the boy's hand casually, "we'll get along fine anyway. Won't we?" This last question she addressed to the boy who seemed not to have heard it. He continued only to stare at Jude with his unchanging, unwavering blue eyes. Jude was utterly defeated as to what the look meant anymore, but it had begun to work on him more acutely than ever.

"Go," he said. "Leave now. They come out at night mostly, like I said—you have as good a chance as any if you leave right now to find some shelter or something."

The woman pulled the boy by the hand, and the boy finally broke his gaze and turned with the woman and walked out the door.

"God be with them," Jude muttered under his breath as he closed the door behind them.

Then Jude was alone and the house was empty again, although it seemed to be only that, emptiness, and solitude perhaps—not Loneliness, not yet.

Jude picked the skillet up off the floor—it was cold now—and placed it back on the inert stovetop. He set it down loudly and sighed loudly. He cleared his throat loudly and sniffed loudly.

"God be with them, thank you, God," he said, loudly.

There was not Loneliness, not yet—only emptiness, and solitude…

Then from outside of the house, he heard a cry—the woman screaming. He went to the door and opened it. As his eyes adjusted to the afternoon light, he perceived the field, and the line of trees beyond, and nothing else. He walked around the side of the house where a hill sloped downward and there was a cluster of bushes. He did not see anything or hear anything. He realized that he had forgotten his gun.

Then he heard the scream again, and he was able to locate it, back around the other side of the house. He went around and looked again toward the line of trees, the trees from which they always emerged at night. In the distance and in the light, he perceived with some difficulty a dark cluster near the tree line. He ran across the field some distance, away from the house. As he drew closer, he heard the cries again, and at last, he drew near enough to see.

It was a crowd of them. They had emerged early, in the daylight. And they were huddled together, eating. And the screams had ceased.

He did not linger to see if they had both been killed—he assumed that they had—nor did he linger to see how they had been killed, how they had been injured, or outrun, torn apart… Knowing that there was nothing to be done, and afraid that they had seen him, he turned and ran as fast as he could back to the house, leapt inside, and closed and locked the door behind him. He knocked his forehead against the wood door and squeezed shut his eyes.

He was deeply unsettled. What justice demanded was what he had done, yet he felt terribly convicted, as though instead he had just committed a grievous wrong.

"Why?" he said. "Why didn't I—why did I—?"

Suddenly, Loneliness invaded the house and swam in his veins like poison.

"Was it my fault? Should I have had them stay, even though…?"

He dropped to his knees, still pressing his head against the door.

"God," he cried, hoping to dispel the Loneliness, "God, please, hear me—"

Loneliness pressed at him, weighing him down with an almost physical strength.

"I'm doing the best I can, Lord," he said. "I'm a changed man, I'm a good man…"

Nothing happened. He attempted for a moment to feel all of the vacant spaces and empty doorways as though they were only that: empty. And he tried to purge his desire. But it was not possible. That he felt Loneliness at all was in itself a wish for un-loneliness, and he could not shake it. And so Loneliness was not only just Loneliness, but also deep and terrible longing—a longing that seemed almost to overcome his faith.

And although he had not stayed to look, his head was filled with images of the woman and the boy in distress, or in death. He imagined their bodies twisted and mangled, he imagined them torn and bloody. He imagined Treyvon Marsh or Michael Harris or Arionna Willis sinking their grey teeth and their rotten gums into their bodies. He had a fleeting thought that this would stave them off for a while, but he knew that even after they had devoured the bodies, they would not be satisfied. They would come for him again, and soon.

He turned his body, leaning his back against the door, tipping his head back and closing his eyes. He felt exhausted. He was beginning to get hungry again, but he wanted to conserve food, and he had wasted a whole extra can. He decided to forgo eating.

He had done it before, and his hunger had always subsided after long enough. This time, though, he feared for some reason that it would not.

He managed to wait until the early evening, when the sun had begun to set and the light coming in through the cracks had faded from a warm yellow to a gentle, dying orange. His hunger was too great, probably because of his exertion and adrenaline during the day, so at last, he rose and went to the door.

Opening the door, he walked out into the fading sunlight and the evening air, which, strangely, seemed not to have cooled much at all. He walked around the side of the house with a vague intention of retrieving more food from the shed, although he already had food in the house. It was more like a habit, or a tic—he merely wanted to see it, to assure himself that it was there.

He rounded the corner and approached the doors to the cellar, but then stopped abruptly.

The padlock was open.

His mind raced, and he thought quickly back to the last time that he had closed it—right after the boy had opened it, mysteriously, and he had closed it hastily in distress. Had he been in too great a hurry, and not closed the padlock firmly enough to fasten it? Had he forgotten to close it altogether? He ran toward it to inspect it.

A small noise alerted him and interrupted these thoughts, but before he had time to process the sound or even fully comprehend that he had heard it at all, the doors burst open.

The horde was crouching inside—the faces of his past: Treyvon Marsh, Michael Harris, Arionna Willis, and *the woman*.

They had been inside the cellar.

They had been waiting for him.

Then they rushed out at him all at once. He turned and fled, knowing that he only hoped to succeed in outrunning them because he was already much closer to the door of the house than they were. He tumbled inside and slammed the door on them, and they seemed to collapse on it the very instant that he did. He fell back onto the floor. Their hands hammered on the door, the walls, the boarded-up windows.

The hammering seemed to shake the house from all around. He crawled backwards away from the door and walls and windows to the middle of the room. He waited. He did not feel any safer at this distance than he would have had he been right up against the wall. Then, the realization slowly came to him that the floor itself was vibrating.

They were underneath him.

They had penetrated the cellar, and it had given them an avenue into the crawlspaces below the floors. They were no longer attacking the house; they had broken through, they were infesting it. There were no barriers left.

With a terrible rending creak, the nails tore from the wood, the boards bent and snapped, and they broke through from under the floor. Their bodies of corruption erupted out of shattered fragments of the gray wood. The house shook violently, its entire structure weakened, as though it were no longer even connected to the ground.

Their breach through the floor seemed to weaken the integrity of the rest of the house. The walls rocked and shook. The plywood rattled and broke away from the windows and the bold angry red light of the evening burst through, flooding the room.

All of the familiar distorted faces leered in at him from the vacant windows and up over the cavity in the floor. Their hands reached up and took hold of what remained of the floor, and their unnatural bodies climbed up. At the windows, they stuck their legs in and climbed over. They moaned and gnashed their teeth, breathing and snarling and gibbering in senseless hunger. Their vacant eyes sought him out and fixed on him. They coalesced into an indeterminate horde and then separated again, approaching as neither individuals nor as a collective. They drove him deeper into the house, back into the kitchen and still further back, filling the house with the pollution of their dark bodies.

At last, he scrambled to his feet and turned to flee, but they knocked him down again and he fell backwards against the refrigerator. Their cold, mortifying fingers clutched at his feet and his ankles, and he kicked at them violently and gripped the floor with the palms of his hands, pushing himself back. He kicked one in the face, driving it back into the crowd, but others descended upon him, grasping at his legs. He kicked against the floor to get away, finding himself now on the tile floor of the bathroom. The boards were still in place over the bathroom window and he was plunged into near darkness. He reached for the porcelain base of the sink and pulled at it, drawing his feet and ankles away from them, and heaving his body upwards. One of them clambered in through the narrow doorway to the bathroom and sank its fingers into the flesh of his arm, piercing the tattooed skin, mangling the name written in ink so that it was unintelligible and then nonexistent. He pulled himself up and away violently, gripping the sink. At his weight, the bowl pulled away from the wall and he fell, breathing dust. He felt suffocated in the darkness, as though he were being buried in somewhere cold, underground.

Others poured in through the door and the weight of them pressed against him, throwing him back against the wall by the showerhead, and with a tremendous crash, they forced him through. The drywall cracked and crumbled, and one of his shoulders struck against a stud in the wall while the other fell freely through the back of the wall, driven back by the pressure. His body turned and he landed on his shoulder on the floor on the other side, back in the living room which was now thick with them. Now frantic beyond all hope and reason, he flailed wildly as their teeth and fingers tore at the flesh of his limbs, kept back only by the violence of his motion, unable yet to get a firm grip on him. His skin was torn and had begun to peel away, and strands of flesh frayed out from the bulk of his arms. Blood fell onto his body from his outstretched hands, spattering his face and chest.

Then they were upon him, a great number of them, pushing down on his body. The force and the pressure cracked his ribs, and at the same moment, the floor underneath him cracked. The whole house shook, and he fell a little ways below into the crawlspace on top of shattered fragments of the floor, his arms splayed out to the side and the sharp, broken wood dug into his arms from underneath them.

He was underneath the cross, which was still hanging high up on the dark wall. At his sudden crash, the cross shook off of its nail and fell. His hands were waving about blindly, in unmeasured motion that was not really the result of any sort of rational thought. His gesture was haphazard, and the cross seemed to find its way into his hand despite his frenzy, and with the last of his strength, he took hold of the cross as tightly as he could. The points of the cross pierced his hand, and the sharp pain of gripping it so tightly seemed to numb the pain of the horde pressing on him as they stopped his flailing, seizing his head and torso and tearing his clothes, tearing his skin, cracking his bones. It was as though it had sent a bolt of energy and a last burst of life through him, blurring his vision of all of the faces that had tormented him for so long.

***

The sun set lazily, fat and red on the horizon as if engorged, and a hush descended on the little house and the plain of dry, whispering grass surrounding it. The house was empty, and the air outside was still and cool. A lone grasshopper took flight, snapping its wings and rattling in the silence only momentarily. As night fell, a chorus of cricket voices rose from within the dark, towering trees, filling the dome of the sky with singing.

THE PENULTIMATE

Nine days had passed since their father had left them. He had left them before, but he had never been gone longer than three days until now.

"He'll be back," Nikki said. "He always comes back."

"But he never takes this long," said Danny. "Something must have happened or he wouldn't have taken this long."

"He never told us that he wouldn't ever be gone longer than three days. Remember, all he said was, 'wait for me; I'll be back.' You know that might mean that even if he takes a long time, he might come back. We just have to wait."

"I'm sure he meant like three or four days. That's all he's ever been gone before. Not *nine*."

"You don't know that's what he meant."

"I'm pretty sure that's what he meant. And I'm pretty sure he's dead by now."

Nikki sat against an empty spot of the wall next to a long-derelict refrigeration unit with her knobby knees drawn up to her face and her skinny arms linked loosely around them. Danny faced her from the opposite wall next to an empty candy rack near the checkstand counter. He sat on a box, strumming an acoustic guitar. He was strumming the same riffs he had been strumming for months—from what seemed so long ago, back when they had been in high school together.

They had taken shelter in a gas station convenience store that lay in between towns. They had driven there on an empty tank, hoping to refuel, but there had been no gas left in the pumps, so they had stayed out of necessity. There were others who had stayed there too. Their father had reasoned that it was as good a place as any, because it was stocked well with food, and the more people who were with them, the safer they would be. However, the number meant that the food ran out fairly quickly and all but their family had eventually left in search of other food and shelter. It was then that their mother had fallen sick and died. Then she had awakened in the monstrous form of the things that attacked and devoured. Their father had not been prepared for it, and it was only after a needlessly long and brutal struggle that he finally crushed her skull and immobilized her. He hadn't spoken for days after that. And when he finally had, a profound change had taken place. He began to speak often and at length about death. He spoke too about the spreading affliction and had deduced that it was demonic in nature.

Their father had never been a religious or spiritual man, so this change had taken both Nikki and Danny by surprise. Nikki had shown deference, listening at first out of sympathy, but finally coming to understand him and even agreeing with some of his ideas. Danny listened more out of a numb respect, neither agreeing nor disagreeing, but simply allowing the space for his father to talk.

Amidst all the talk, Danny had grown restless and worried that his father's lack of action might lead to their undoing. The gas station in which they were holed up was near a military base which covered a vast amount of property, mostly still undeveloped forest. Danny had brought up the proximity of the base and the likelihood that they might find safety, shelter, and other survivors there, but his father had dismissed the idea.

"You sound like you don't care," Nikki said. "You sound like you're happy if he's dead."

Nikki was the older of the two—she was twenty. Danny, on the cusp of turning nineteen, wore a full beard and was stoutly built, and Nikki had always been very thin, so to look at them, Danny seemed the older until by dint of their interactions their age and relationship became evident.

"I'm not. I'm just pretty sure he is dead."

Danny had been nursing the dream of becoming a guitar player in a band for years, although he lacked the discipline to practice often. It was only now that they had seemingly limitless time on their hands, and no electricity with which he could listen to the music that he enjoyed, he had actually begun to play regularly. He was rehearsing, perfecting the riffs, and honing his technique. Unfortunately, however, it seemed that playing in a band would not be happening any time soon. Oh, well, he told himself. Society will rebuild itself eventually. There will be time.

Nikki tired of his playing it over and over, and of the repetitiveness of the riff itself, but it also reminded her of home, of family, of their previous life. For this reason, she enjoyed it in a certain sense, although she was afraid that since he played it now more than ever before, she would come to associate it with their current circumstance, like everything else.

"Well, you sound relieved or something," she said.

Danny stopped at his playing and put the guitar to the side. "I'm not relieved. I don't hope he's dead. I guess I'm just… numb. I dunno."

Nikki said nothing for a while. She set her long, thin face—which had grown even longer and thinner in the past months—down against her knees and inhaled through the fabric.

Danny began strumming again.

"I'm worried," Nikki said at last.

"Well, what do you want to do?"

"What do you mean?" Nikki said.

"Well, you can sit here and worry as much as you want, but it's not going to change—"

He broke off, unsure of his words, giving her instead a knowing look that communicated what he hoped she already understood.

Nikki's eyes were cloudy with tears. She nodded and looked down again. "Maybe you're right," she said. "Maybe he is—" She laid her skinny hands to the sides of her head, gripping it through her thin hair. "I just can't believe—"

Danny stopped strumming the guitar again and laid it by. He knew that she was mulling over everything that their father had said about death. "One of us will live to see the other two dead," he had reminded them. "I pray that it's not me, but the way things are—who can tell?" He had said that he spoke to them often of death because it was important to remember, but the more he did it, and the more Danny thought about it, the more he thought that he spoke about death because he was still grieving the loss of their mother, and it was his way of processing it, of dealing with the pain. So he had begun to dismiss the words. But the words had come home. And now both Nikki and Danny were wondering who would be the second-to-last, and who would be the last. And if it were only a matter of time, then perhaps it was time that was of the essence.

"How long do you think we should wait for him?" Danny said at last.

"I don't know," said Nikki, choking back the beginnings of tears and sniffing her nose. "He said to wait for him. He said that it wasn't about the time, that he would be back no matter what… that it would seem like a long time to us, but that he would be back. Don't you remember him saying that?"

"Yeah, I do. I do, but…" Danny shook his head.

"Maybe one more day?" Nikki said hopefully.

Danny nodded. "Okay."

"And then what?" asked Nikki.

"I want to try the military base."

"I don't know," she said. "It might be dangerous trying to go over there. I don't know what Dad would think of that."

"I think it's probably our best chance," Danny replied.

"But we don't know what kind of people they are. Maybe there are bad people there. We might get killed on the way."

"Well, we're out of food here. It's not doing us any good just sitting around. I think it will be safe. It's an Army base—they probably had it all locked down right from the start. I don't know why we didn't go there before. Dad was just afraid for no reason."

"Don't say that."

"Okay, okay, but if he had a reason, I don't know what it was. Because they're 'demonic' or whatever. Doesn't make a difference, really. To be honest, I don't really remember much of what he said. Anyway, I'm sure it's stocked full of food, and they're Army guys; they know how to defend themselves. They will be able to keep us safe. Safer than we'll be here when they find us. Those things will smash right through those glass windows. I don't know why they haven't found us here already. We must have just been really lucky so far. It's only a matter of time."

Nikki looked around the store at the empty shelves, the dark refrigerators. "I don't know about the Army base. I just don't know."

"They're *trained* to keep people safe. It's probably the safest place there is as long as we can make it there."

"How can they keep us safe? How do you know they can keep us safe?"

"I'm sure they know a lot more than we do. I'm sure they've figured out a lot more than Dad figured out... raving about them being demonic and shit. Look, I love Dad, but after Mom—after he had to kill Mom—I think he kind of lost it a little. That's also partially why I think he's not coming back."

"How can you say that?"

"He said that they were demonic! What more do you need? It will be nice to be in the hands of the U.S. Government. It will be nice to be in the hands of somebody else, people who are neutral, who don't tell you how to think. They won't turn us away, at least."

Nikki gave in. "Okay," she said. "After we give him one more day, we'll go. We'll go and try to get in that military base."

"Tomorrow morning," Danny said. "If he doesn't show up by tomorrow morning, we go."

Nikki nodded.

Danny picked up his guitar and started strumming again, more loudly now that they were no longer trying to carry on a conversation. They spent the remainder of the day like that—Nikki sitting against the wall, and Danny strumming the guitar. At the slightest movement outside—the flicker of a bird flying past, the shadow of a cloud passing over the sun—they would look up with alert eyes, hoping for the return of their father. At other times, they would hear a noise—the scuttle of a creature clambering along the vacant shelves, or the rattle of a bird living in the ceiling—and their hearts would race, their hands would go numb, and they would brace for their total inability to fight whatever impending doom might befall them. But in the case of both the great hope and the great fear, they were met with indifferent nothingness. It always ended where it had started: with just the two of them, waiting.

Before long, Danny was stricken with a pang of hunger, and he knew that in an hour or two it would pass, and that then it would be time to sleep. Nikki got up and walked to the front of the store and lay behind the counter where she slept.

"Do you mind if I keep playing?" Danny asked.

"No, not really," said Nikki from behind the counter.

"'Not really'? You mean, you sort of do mind?"

"Well—"

"You mean, you *mostly* mind, don't you?"

"I don't want you to stop on my account. I know that you enjoy it."

"Shut up. I'll stop. Go to sleep. I know you're tired."

"Okay. Thank you. Good night."

"Good night," said Danny, hunger jabbing at him from within. He laid the guitar down beside him and tipped his head back and closed his eyes. He was tired, but the hunger would keep him awake for some time yet. He moved his fingers in the air, practicing on a silent, invisible guitar.

***

They awoke in the early morning, restless from hunger and waiting for their father. He had not returned.

"Give him another couple of hours," Nikki said.

"Okay," said Danny.

He could tell that she was on the verge of tears. It seemed that she was too exhausted to cry. If she had had food enough for the energy, she would have been weeping.

They waited. He did not come.

So in the mid-morning, they set out. The only thing they took with them was Danny's guitar which he carried on his back by a strap wrapped around one shoulder. The morning was cool—a layer of clouds covered the sky, partially diffusing and muting the sunlight.

They walked along a main road, scattered sparsely with empty, dead cars. Stoplights hung dark on their wires. The windows of shops were empty and dark. Most of the houses were boarded up. Those that were not were dark and appeared to be empty. All was quiet and motionless. They felt all alone.

"Where do you think they all are?" Nikki whispered as they walked.

"Who—people or… or the others?"

Nikki didn't answer his question, but looked around as though the only way to account for the desolation of their surroundings was that invisible strangers were all about her, who might appear at any instant. She kept a hopeful eye out for her father, but Danny was not as optimistic. He was watchful for other things.

Once, she stopped and pointed at an empty storefront, saying, "Is that him? I think it's him!"

Danny looked. The storefront was dark and looked as empty as all the others.

"I don't see anything," he said.

"But don't you see—" she said, "the windows are covered with newspaper, just like Dad does. There are doors on both sides of the building, and on the front, just like the last place, just like how Dad says is the safest—more exits, more ways to get away. And it's a convenience store, not a market, so it will have more non-perishables."

Danny studied the building. "You're right about all those things. But it doesn't mean he's inside. Those aren't signs of him, those are just external things about the building. They don't mean anything."

"But it's *exactly* the sort of place he would be."

"Still doesn't mean anything."

"But what if it is?"

"If it is Dad, what is he doing—why would he be hiding out instead of trying to make his way back to us? Did he abandon us? If he's actually in there, that means he's abandoned us and he doesn't care about us, so I wouldn't want to go there even if he *were* there."

"Maybe he's just waiting for the right moment. Maybe he's trying to figure out—" Nikki floundered for words, and then gave up. She felt despair. She did not see a way that she could convince Danny. It seemed as though his mind had already been made up about their father, and that any evidence she provided he could always justifiably dismiss.

"Well," she said, "even if it's not Dad in there, there are probably helpful people."

"You said we shouldn't trust anyone except Dad. Besides, we have to try to make it to the base before dark."

"I know, but…maybe they could help us. Maybe they have some food they could spare."

"Give it up, Nikki," said Danny, turning on her. "They might be helpful, but they might not. They might not even be people in there anymore. Maybe *they're* locked *inside* and we should keep it that way. We have to play it safe. We need to act as though we're on our own, because, for all practical concern, we are. We're on our own, Nikki. We're all alone, until we get to that base, or unless Dad miraculously shows up, which he won't."

They continued walking. Nikki still kept her eye out. She saw other places and other signs that indicated the presence of their father, that he was still alive. But she kept these to herself, knowing that it was useless to talk to Danny.

Danny saw none of these signs. All he saw was the desolation that surrounded them, and this to him was proof enough that their father was dead.

They took breaks more frequently as the day wore on, the hunger getting to them. They thought more than once to stop at a vacant convenience store or an empty restaurant along the way, but they feared that these were either inhabited by others who might be hostile, or that they were infested, so they kept moving in hopes of reaching the gates to the base before dark.

They succeeded, and they arrived not long before sunset at one of the gates on the road. The booth at the checkpoint was vacant and the board guarding the entrance from the road had been broken. The car that had apparently broken through it lay not far from the gate, turned on its side like a dead insect near the edge of the pavement against a grassy ditch. They walked down the road beyond the overturned car and passed another convenience store— also dark, vacant. The base looked as desolate as everything else they had seen.

Then as they rounded the curve in the road, they came to the large, flat expanse of the main campus of the base. Several old-fashioned buildings lay squat in a formation amid overgrown landscaping plants. There were few windows in the buildings and it was impossible to tell if they were occupied.

They continued walking farther down the road toward a large, mall-like building that they saw in the distance, standing at the center of a large, flat, empty parking lot expanse. As they drew closer to the building, they saw tall, thin structures in front, like flagpoles without flags, that became thicker toward the top. Something about the building seemed to beckon them—perhaps its size, and its apparent centrality to the base—so they walked toward it.

The sun had set behind the building, and in the early period of its absence, the sky and clouds had discolored in blotches of red and purple, like bruises. As they drew closer to the building, they saw that the structures in front were not flagpoles at all, but tall wooden poles that stood at slight angles, not exactly parallel to each other or perpendicular to the ground. They were topped with short, horizontal boards that made each into the shape of a T, and hung on each by the board at the top were human forms.

At the sight of it, they slowed their pace next to each other. Nikki's heart leapt into her throat and she pulled at Danny's hand. Although Danny was also fear-stricken, he tightened his grip on her and led her forward with him. They continued their approach, stepping from the road onto the sidewalk, crossing through a shaggy hedge, and walking out onto the paved expanse of the empty parking lot. Except for clumps of fallen leaves and other debris, the parking lot was in surprisingly good shape. There were no cracks in the pavement, and the paint was still clearly visible.

As they drew closer to the poles, they saw that the forms hung to the tops of the T's were not humans, but emaciated figures of the undead. Their skin had tightened around their forms so that they appeared vaguely skeletal, and the skin, dried out and withered, had turned dark. They were motionless, and appeared 'dead.' Neither Danny nor Nikki had ever witnessed the creatures dying except through severe injury, and this sight, although it showed them to have been essentially subdued and no longer presenting a threat, still terrified and sickened them. They were not sure if these things could 'suffer,' but the image created a spontaneous feeling of empathy in them both. Danny dismissed this quickly with the thought that this must have been *done* by someone. They demonstrated a great power possessed by some person or force—presumably, whoever was inside the building. They would be very safe, indeed.

"Let's go," said Danny, pulling Nikki's hand, and now beginning to feel a giddy excitement and relief.

Nikki was still transfixed in unthinking horror at the figures, but Danny's pull at her wrist awakened her somewhat, and she followed him. They walked underneath the poles, and approached what appeared to be the main doors of the building. They were large, gray metal doors, windowless. Danny pulled at the handle on one of the doors. The door was locked. He rapped his fist on it.

When nothing happened, Danny doubted that there was anyone on the base at all, and feared that their entire journey was for nothing, that whoever had bound the creatures to the poles out front had long since died or moved on.

Just then, there was a rattling as of chains or other metal binding on the other side of the door. Instinctively, Danny and Nikki both drew back. The latch clicked heavily and the door opened a crack. The interior appeared dimly lit from the slit in the doorway, and a dark face looked out from within and brandished a large assault rifle. Upon looking at them, the figure, a woman, leveled the rifle at them.

"Get lost," she said.

Nikki's throat caught and she was prepared to turn and leave, but Danny spoke up.

"Please," he said. "We need help. We ran out of food, and we walked all day to get here…"

"Fuck off. I'll give you one last warning."

"Please—" he said again. "We don't know where else to go… We thought that, since you were the Army…"

The woman held the rifle steady but did not fire. She looked back and forth at the two of them.

"Take the bag off and put it on the ground and open it—slow."

Danny had nearly forgotten that he had been wearing the guitar on his back. Trembling, but knowing that he did not have anything to fear, he took it off and set it on the ground. Slowly, as he had been instructed, he unzipped the case revealing the guitar inside.

"Were you followed?"

Danny looked about himself as though she had asked him if anything were stuck to his clothing.

"I don't think so," he said. "At least, we didn't see—"

"Bullshit, you got followed. I ought to leave you out here."

Nikki felt on the verge of tears, but the woman lifted her gun and motioned for them to get inside. Danny picked up his guitar and went in first, and Nikki followed. The woman ushered her in, grabbing her arm and practically throwing her inside with such a force that Nikki nearly fell. They were in a small chamber, like an anteroom, with a hallway that led around a corner. The woman closed the heavy outer door. Laying her gun to the side, she wrapped a long chain around the handles of the door, looping it several times, and then replaced a heavy iron bar across the doors.

She retrieved her rifle and turned to face them, her posture aggressive.

"Walk," she said.

Danny started walking down the hallway, looking back at her before he rounded the corner as if for confirmation. She did nothing, so he continued.

The hallway was long and narrow with cream-colored walls. As they walked, they passed a space in the wall that led to bathrooms labeled MEN'S and WOMEN'S. They continued down the hall until its end, where they emerged in a large open space.

It was like a small shopping mall, with high ceilings and long walkways lined with shops, lit dimly with the dusk only by skylights far above. Their steps echoed through it as though it were a church. The woman directed them to turn left and continue down a long row of shops. All of the windows and signs were still intact, and except that they were unlit, they looked nothing out of the ordinary.

She stopped them in front of a furniture store.

"Here," she said.

They entered; it was a large store that resembled more of a warehouse than a retail space. Faux walls built for display created half rooms connected by maze-like turns. The lights were on— harsh fluorescent lights that hummed far above them. Somewhere deep within among the faux rooms, a voice murmured in low conversation.

"Lieutenant," the woman barked.

The conversation stopped, and after a moment a stooped, pale man emerged from around a corner.

"Couple a kids," she said.

The man looked them up and down and said, "Reepus know?"

"No."

"You give 'em the test?"

"No. They just got here."

"Well, let's give 'em the test."

"Yes, sir." Then, turning to the children, she ordered, "Sit."

Looking about them, Danny and Nikki each chose a chair out of the furniture that was nearby, while the lieutenant disappeared around the corner again. Danny dropped the guitar case off of his shoulder onto the floor next to his chair.

They were tired from walking. Almost as soon as he had sat, Danny's stomach clenched painfully. He was lightheaded and weak, and the room seemed to recede from him for an instant. He looked over at Nikki and saw that she had her hands over her face, not in sadness, but in exhaustion. It seemed that she could no longer hold her own head up without the support of her hands.

Danny could not tell how long the lieutenant was gone, but after what seemed a very long time, he returned with two pieces of paper bearing dense, dark handwriting.

"All right," he said, addressing them both. Nikki lifted her head from her hands and looked at him with bleary eyes. "You are in the hands of the United States Army. If you are United States citizens or can pass a simple citizenship test, you are entitled to all of the rights and protection of United States citizenship. At this time, the unit that I represent is in a state of high alert due to the fact that we are currently without communication or correspondence with the central government of the United States. As such, we have necessarily assumed a temporary sovereignty in regards to executive, legislative, and judicial governance and exercise whatever measures and/or precautions including the precaution of the gathering of evidence supporting citizenship or the eligibility thereto deemed necessary to protect and enforce said sovereignty in full accordance and compliance with United States constitutional law insofar as such measures and/or precautions have not altered, added, or removed said United States constitutional law such as persists in material and/or immaterial form at this location and/or vis a vis persons possessed of such knowledge. My name is Lieutenant Dennis Wheeler, and I will be guiding you through the process."

He extended his hand first to Danny. Danny returned the gesture and Lieutenant Wheeler shook it abruptly and then turned to Nikki. Nikki also returned the gesture, holding out her thin white hand, which Lieutenant Wheeler shook as though it were a fish that he had just caught and were attempting to subdue.

"Now, then," he said. "Do you have your social security card, driver's license, and/or birth certificate, or some other form of identification with which I can confirm your identities as citizens of the United States?"

They looked at each other blankly. Nikki shook her head, and Danny shook his.

"All right then, not to worry, not to worry," the lieutenant said. "I have here a simple test with which you can still identify that you are eligible for citizenship. If passed successfully, you will still be provided with all of the support and protection provided to citizens of the United States as part of the emergency measures lawfully adopted and amended to constitutional law by the unit that I represent."

"Okay," said Danny. Nikki nodded.

"Okay," echoed Lieutenant Wheeler, handing one of the papers to each of them, along with a pencil. "No cheating!" he added with a smile.

Danny and Nikki exchanged another glance and then set to work. Danny placed the paper on his lap and examined the questions. The first few were easy enough: he knew that the declaration of independence declared the states' independence from Britain; that freedom of religion means that you can practice any religion or none at all; that separation of church and state means that the state will not force its beliefs on anyone; and that all citizens have the same rights because of the belief that all men are created equal. But there were others that were more difficult: he could not name his state's senator or one of its representatives; he did not know how many amendments the constitution had; and he did not know the date of the last day when he could send in his federal income tax return. After several of these kinds of questions, he gave up and handed the paper back to Lieutenant Wheeler with a sneer of disgust. The lieutenant smiled an automatic smile and took it from him. Nikki was deep in thought over hers, cradling her head with one hand, and tapping the pencil against her mouth with the other.

Danny was overcome with fatigue and his hunger had subsided, so he leaned into one of the sides of his chair and let his eyes fall shut. The instant his eyes closed, the world seemed to spin away from him, and he was lost in a gray velvet ether of non-vision. The hum of the lights and the soft reverberations of the room seemed to lull him instantly to sleep.

He had not slept long when he was awakened by the scuffle of Nikki returning her test to the lieutenant. Danny opened his eyes and looked up. The lieutenant was running his eyes back and forth between each of them, checking the answers of each at the same time. He held his hand down at one point on Danny's, and continued on with Nikki's alone. Then he stopped at a point on hers as well and looked up.

"I'm sorry," he said. "But I'm afraid you do not meet the qualifications that would entitle you to protection from the United States Army." He looked at Danny. "The last day to return your federal income tax return is… the fifteenth of April." Danny shrugged and tipped his head back. Lieutenant Wheeler looked at Nikki. "There are twenty-*nine* amendments to the constitution."

Nikki's face twisted in shock. "*What?*" she exclaimed.

"Twenty-nine."

"No, there aren't—there are twenty-seven!" she said, sitting forward in her chair and staring at the man.

"Since this unit has necessarily assumed a temporary sovereignty in regards to executive, legislative, and judicial governance and exercises whatever measures and/or precautions deemed necessary to protect said sovereignty, this unit has accordingly amended the constitution as it has seen fit in pursuance of this goal."

"But—how was I supposed to know that? And, can you even *do* that?"

"I'm sorry. Everyone is given an equal opportunity. All of the amendments and legislation enacted by this unit have been instated only through constitutionally lawful and democratic processes. Now, although we cannot afford you the protection, service, and amenities that we would to United States citizens or those otherwise eligible, we have arranged for a provisional holding space where you can stay with others in a similar situation. I can present your case to the commander of the unit, General Reepus, if you would like. The general is—" Lieutenant Wheeler broke off and his eyes wandered upward in thought. His previous speech had rolled out of him with almost machine-like automaticity, so this break of silence had the effect of a gunshot. "Well, you will simply have to meet him. The general is the general. He has... well, for my part, he has enlarged *my* mind. You will have to meet him. In any case, I can speak to him on your behalf, if you wish."

Nikki's eyes were red-rimmed and clouded with tears. Her face was dark and sunken with fatigue. "Yes, please," she replied weakly.

The lieutenant rose. "Then I will leave you with Sergeant Taylor." Then he turned and left them alone with the woman who had initially escorted them in. Danny let his eyes close again. Nikki looked at the woman, Sergeant Taylor.

"How many of you are here?" Nikki asked her.

Taylor looked at her with unflinching eyes, clutching her rifle at attention, and did not respond.

"Why are those—those things outside? On the crosses?"

Taylor sighed as though reluctant to answer, but said, "They fear the smell of their own dead. General Reepus made the discovery. It's how we've survived."

"How did he discover that?" Nikki asked.

Taylor tilted her head and glared. "He's a *great* man," she hissed, her words issuing like flames from her mouth.

Lieutenant Wheeler appeared from around the same corner and approached Danny and Nikki.

"He won't see you," he said, "but he's instructed me to lead you to the holding room."

Danny lifted his head and opened his eyes. Nikki looked relieved, but the lieutenant's voice had sounded tired—as though he didn't really believe the good news he had relayed.

"If you'll follow me, please," he said.

Nikki rose from her chair. Danny shook himself awake and rose slowly from the chair. He reached down and picked up his guitar, slung the strap over his shoulder, and walked lazily after the other two. Taylor cast a wicked glare at them as though she intended to spit on them as they passed. Danny wondered what the reason was for such ire—perhaps it was because they hadn't met the requirements for citizenship. Perhaps she hated them because she felt that they had taken advantage of, or had not truly understood, the privileges they had previously enjoyed as citizens. In any case, he felt that an unfair barrier had been set up between them, that she was acting irrationally.

Lieutenant Wheeler led them out of the furniture store back into the main walkway of the mall, which was now dark with night. He turned on a flashlight which cast a dim, ominous glow before them, a glow which, when cast far ahead into the depth of the hallway, disappeared into the darkness. Their footsteps echoed loudly through the building, the whispering returns of sound playing at their ears, suggesting the sounds of others—perhaps the other citizens, or those eligible for the same protection—or perhaps something else altogether, hiding in the dark, waiting for an opportunity to strike.

After they had walked for some length, the beam of the flashlight grew dim, and flickered.

"Fuck," muttered the lieutenant, shaking the light in his hand. The light flickered at his shaking it, eventually giving out and plunging them into darkness. "Oh, well," he said. "We're nearly there. Stick close to me. Here—let's hold hands."

Danny stretched out his hand in the dark and waved it about, eventually making contact with Nikki's, and then after another brief waving about of hands, they were all three connected. They walked forward in a chain, as though in a dance, and in the pitch darkness, although there were only the three of them, Danny felt as if he may as well have been at the end of a chain made up of the entire remnant of humanity, interminably long and led forward through total darkness toward a destination of deep, unfathomable gloom by a distant, unseen master.

"Going down," said the lieutenant. Danny braced himself for the stairs but stumbled anyway, nearly tumbling forward and losing his grip on Nikki, onto which he held as though her hand were a lifeline.

They came to a landing, and in the distance there was a narrow, horizontal slit of light—the crack at the bottom of a door. They walked toward this, bringing themselves up to it and then standing in waiting. In the dim light, Danny could begin to make out the vague forms of his other companions. The lieutenant undid a chain and a latch on the door that sounded almost as extensive as those that had guarded entry through the main door of the building. Then, with a creak of metal hinges, the heavy door swung open.

The room was dimly lit from a single overhead bulb that cast a harsh beam downward. The floor was littered with indeterminate debris and in the middle of this was a naked man sitting on the floor directly below the light. His head hung down so that all but the top of the crown and the backs of his bare shoulders were in shadow. Cords or strands of something fell from bracelets at his wrists. At their entrance, the head lifted up slowly to look at them, the face still in shadow.

Danny took in these surroundings, acclimating himself to the idea of this as his new place of habitation, but following this, the man's head lifted a little more, and the light fell on it, and Danny's perception changed as if a curtain had been lifted from his eyes.

The face was not human, but inhuman—pale, sickly, ravaged by decay, one eye sunken in and blind, the other staring out from the face with a cold, almost glowing intensity. The dark pieces of debris scattering the floor were human remains—bones and fragments of bones, brown with rot and old dry flesh.

Almost at the same moment of Danny's realization, Lieutenant Wheeler threw Nikki forward savagely by the neck. She flew toward the creature, landing on her hands and knees, clattering among the bones.

Then, before Danny had a chance to react, the lieutenant hit him in the side with a blow so sharp that it sent him to the floor doubled over in pain. The lieutenant knelt over Danny, removing the strap to the guitar case and flinging it aside. He pulled Danny's hands behind his back and bound them with a nylon cable.

At Nikki's collapse, the creature leapt up, the chains attached to its bracelets clattering, and it rushed at Nikki's fallen form. Nikki was too tired and hungry to move quickly, and the creature was upon her while she was still struggling to get up from her knees. It seized her head with its hands and gripped it with terrifying strength. Nikki screamed in agony. The creature tightened its grip and cracked her skull with the pressure. A circle of blood resembling a crown had formed around her head where the skin had broken and ran down into her eyes and stung them. Her body writhed and her fingers clutched wildly at the creature. Her motion intensified, gradually becoming spasmodic as the creature tore away the skull from her brain and plunged its ravenous mouth into the bowl of it, and then she suddenly stopped, and her body fell limp.

The lieutenant hoisted the bound Danny back up to his feet. Danny looked toward the creature and watched as it finished devouring the last of Nikki's brains and moved on to the meat of her. It ate ravenously, as they always did, although watching it from this vantage—like watching a creature in a zoo—made it seem almost natural; it ate as he expected a starved animal might eat. It huddled over the body of its prey, back arched and head bent down, the arms hanging low and the skeletal hands grasping at flesh as only a secondary means of tearing it from the bone and rending it apart, the primary being the teeth and jaws bathed with thick swaths of blood. With its unnaturally strong arms, it worked the joints of Nikki's limbs backwards, cracking the weaker bones and snapping the ligaments so that the limbs came apart and separated from the body. It held them high above with its hands and sucked the blood that drained onto its face, and then consumed the skin and muscle. It took no great care to avoid the clothing in its haste, only removing it when it presented an obstacle that could not be otherwise overcome. It became especially zealous over the intestines, which it pulled out of the body like cord and attempted to stuff into its mouth all at once even though the slippery tubes resisted it. Danny watched the fiend finish her off to the bone until, at the end, it scooped out her eyes with its fingers and ate them pensively and almost reluctantly, popping and crunching them deliberately between its teeth and slowly sucking them down.

Then Danny felt at his back a firm pressure—the lieutenant's hand, urging him forward.

The creature looked up languidly, its one good eye a little slower, less alert than it had been earlier.

Danny resisted the push and scrambled to move backwards, but slipped on a bone and fell.

"Don't make this difficult," said the lieutenant.

Danny was too weak to do much, and the lieutenant dragged him forward. The creature stood, stooped over like a vulture, arms hanging limply, hands lifted slightly in expectation.

The lieutenant threw Danny forward, nearly onto the remains of Nikki. The creature, moving more slowly now, bent over him. Danny could smell the metallic aroma of blood and the rank stench of the half-rotting thing and the pollution of its breath.

It lowered its head, and Danny was closer to it than he had ever been to one before. He observed the ruggedness of its desiccated, leathery skin, the blue-green areas of the skin where moisture still remained, and the black cavity of the nose where the flesh was missing, either rotted off or torn off at some point during its rough existence. The one good eye looked at him coldly and without movement, seeming to glow from some sort of lurid inner illumination, and at the same time, to draw light into itself, as though it were glowing with darkness itself. It spread its thin, taut lips up and over blackening teeth and dark, shrunken gums to reveal its horrid jaws, and it dipped its head toward him. Then it sank its rotten teeth into his shoulder. Danny's vision blurred and once again the world felt as though it were spinning away from him, and he had the vague sensation of being pulled backward, dragged away from the creature, and then he sank into fatigue, delirium, and despair, and all was dark.

***

Out of the darkness, there was a *voice*—a pulsating stream of sound that formed words that were as yet beyond comprehension. Gradually, other senses came, the sense of darkness, the sense of the weight of a body, and then awareness of the self—awareness that it was *he* who sensed. He felt trapped in the body, in the weight of it, unable to send its muscles into motion, or to throw open his eyes.

Then the voice stopped, and he heard another, a smaller, weaker voice, the voice of something more like a human. It seemed very close to him, and he caught at last some snatches of words:

"This one is fat…last a long time…"

Then there was a sharp pain at his wrists as of pressure or burning. At this, he managed to send movement coursing through his body, although it was weak—he doubted if he had actually effected any real movement, or if he had merely produced in himself the sensation of it.

The voice came again, and in Danny's emerging consciousness, he caught bits of the words and phrases that it uttered.

But it was not so much the words and phrases that mattered, but the darkness behind them, darkness that permeated the voice as it spoke, and the words that were spoken by it.

"We must defend…" it said, the voice echoing deeply in the darkness. "We must defend the supreme law of the land. Every law that is ever written implies the value of its own defense. We hold these truths to be self-evident…"

The sense of a dim light came to Danny, and he struggled to open his eyes. At great length, he was able to do so, and found himself looking up at an unfinished warehouse ceiling. The lights directly above him were not on, but there was a distant hum, and he guessed himself to be in another part of the furniture warehouse, not far from where he and Nikki had been earlier.

"In war, a commander must always determine an acceptable loss. A tree…must be pruned, or else it grows too large. Weeds must be removed if all plants are to flourish. In the garden, sacrifices must be made. To create an Eden, one must *introduce* a Fall."

Danny struggled once more to move, and felt the resistance of his body on some surface underneath him which sent sharp pangs of discomfort through his back. His wrists, tied behind him, burned and restricted his movement. He relaxed in his effort to move and fell back, and then was overcome with a wave of nausea. His neck and shoulder ached.

And then in a flood of sensation, the memory of what had happened came to him—the death of Nikki, and the horrible creature leaning down for him—had he been saved? He was alive; his own sense told him that. Where was he? What had happened?

A pang of hunger shot through him, incapacitating him, and mingling with his nausea. Had he had anything in his stomach, he would have vomited—but he was empty. He lay back, submitting to the uncontrollable, roiling pain inside him.

"The mother of the Stegodyphus spider defends her eggs from male spiders who would destroy the eggs because they were not the ones who fertilized the mother. They defend their own fitness, destroying anything not of their own lineage, for genetic domination. But if the mother is victorious... the mother eats them... and then continues to eat... and eats, and eats, consuming beyond comprehension... and when her offspring are born, she regurgitates what she has eaten for her young. The young feed on her vomit... and then they eat *her*. And this species has survived from Eden."

The nausea and the pain of hunger subsided somewhat, and he struggled harder. The more he exerted, the more his wrists burned, and he was unable to move. He realized then that not only had his wrists and ankles been bound, but his whole body was tied down by lengths of cord.

"Fire with fire."

A chill descended on him. His muscles ached.

"Death is a necessary end, and it will come when it will come."

The nausea and the hunger mingled, but he knew them to be distinct. He sputtered for breath and drew his body from side to side searching in vain for a position less painful. He smelled rank flesh, and blood.

"I will have mercy on whom I have mercy, and I will harden whom I harden, in order to make known the riches of my glory, which I have prepared beforehand."

He felt a shuddering motion underneath him, and then the sensation of being lifted up. His wrists burned in agony as the weight of his body shifted. The wound on his shoulder ached terribly.

"*E pluribus unum—annuit cœptis.*"

He was lifted upright by the armpit, his body hanging limply, his feet dangling on floor. From this angle, he saw the maze of false walls and the arrangements of display furniture. He caught a glimpse of a figure just on the edge of his vision to the left, a slight figure from what he could tell, seeming to have no connection with the voice that he had heard, although there was no one else from whom the voice could have come. He strained to look farther over, but could not. Pain gripped his whole body; his insides heaved and pain shot through his arm.

He was carried by the armpits through the maze of walls out into the main hallway, which was now dimly lit again, this time with the light of the coming dawn. He assumed that he was being carried by the two he knew, Lieutenant Wheeler and Sergeant Taylor. He had seen or heard no one else, except for the voice of General Reepus who remained behind within the dark depth of the maze, and as they dragged him through the hall, he saw nothing but the dark shops by the dim blue light of early morning, and heard nothing except for the echoes of the footsteps and the dragging of his own bound feet toward the entrance.

They came to the doors. His right side dropped, and Taylor stepped forward to unchain the handles and remove the bar lock. She took up her assault rifle and cracked the door. Pure blue light bled in through the opening. She stuck her head out and then withdrew, nodding to Wheeler. They hoisted him up again and dragged him out into the cool morning. It was well before sunrise, the day still in its very gestation. They pulled him over the ground up to the row of crosses planted in the ground and dropped him in the dewy grass.

The woman retrieved a ladder that was resting on the side of the building, extended it, and leaned it up against one of the crosses. She climbed up the ladder, a black, lean figure against the glowing blue sky, up to where one of the creatures was hung. She drew a blade from her belt and cut at the rope that tied its feet. Then she climbed a little higher and cut the cord that tied one of its wrists. The arm fell free, and the skin cracked like dry leaves. The body swung off of the main beam of the cross and dangled by the remaining wrist. Then the woman cut the cord and the creature dropped from the cross and landed on the ground, collapsing into itself, bending and breaking like a fallen limb of a tree.

She pocketed the blade and then climbed back down, the metal ladder clattering as she descended. She hooked her arm under Danny's armpit, and Lieutenant Wheeler took hold of his ankles and shuffled to the side, swinging his legs around so that he was in position next to the ladder. The woman pulled him up and Lieutenant Wheeler pushed at his legs.

As they drew him up the ladder, he felt dizzy. The world seemed to sway and rock, and his vision of the blue light of the waking world was flecked with floating swirls of light and dark. His right arm was numb. The transformation was taking hold.

After they had finally dragged him to the top, the woman leaned him against the horizontal board that cut off the vertical, extracted her blade once again, and cut the nylon cable around his wrists. His arms fell loose weakly, the flesh cut and bleeding. She worked fast; she knew that her activity might attract them at any moment. She tied one wrist and then the other around the wooden plank, testing the cord to be sure that it would hold his weight before she let him drop. Then she descended the ladder and wrapped his already bound ankles with cord around the wood.

Danny turned his head to either side, observing his neighbors. One was nearly completely dried; it moved its withered head up and down with great effort, its skin cracked and flaking. The other was still relatively fresh; its eyes were clearer and its skin was the usual purple-blue. He wondered when the poor soul had found the encampment—if it, too, had failed the citizenship test—if it were, like he and Nikki, lost, confused, clinging to a last shred of hope for deliverance.

The woman finished her work and sheathed the blade for the last time. She descended the ladder and then drew it down, leaving Danny strung at the top to complete the transformation and then, like the others, to act as a deterrent. She took the ladder away, leaning it against the building where it had been before, and then she and the lieutenant went back in and sealed the entrance.

Then he was alone with the quiet, blue dawn, and the others next to him whose form had already been transmuted into what he would soon become himself. He looked to the side at his own arm: his flesh was beginning to turn green. He could feel it in his bloodstream; with each pump of his heart, his vision became clouded with darkness, and his hearing obscured. For the first time in his life, he was afraid of his own death.

But aside from the personal fear and avulsion he held toward death, he was unsure how to take it. If there were others inside, other citizens, then he was at peace about his own situation. He understood something of the notion of "the greater good." But this was insufficient to shore up his feelings of loss.

For some reason, as he hung there on the cross, his thoughts kept returning to his father. Was he still alive? Had he abandoned them, or was he still in pursuit, perhaps already returned to the convenience store where they had been?

At that moment, a memory arose in his mind like something bobbing up to the surface of water.

The memory was of his father, and of himself from only a few years ago, when he had been twelve or thirteen. Once, while out and about with his parents, he had happened upon a pet store with a display of impounded puppies that were available for adoption. Among them was a Rottweiler mix. Danny wanted it. At first, his father had objected to the idea because Rottweilers required training, as much or more than any other breed of dog, he said. Danny persisted, arguing that he would undertake to train the dog. Finally, his father had relented, and allowed him to get the puppy provided that he train it; and if he failed, he would have to give the dog away, have it impounded again, or most likely put down.

His father provided him with books on training the dog and read through portions of them with him, even demonstrating some of the techniques himself on the puppy. Danny tried to emulate his father and tried to train the puppy as best he could. But the more he worked, the more stubborn and resistant the puppy seemed to his attempts. He never went to his father about it, but his father knew, and Danny knew that he knew.

Danny went to a camp later that summer. While Danny was away, his father took two weeks off of work and trained the puppy himself. When Danny came back, the puppy acted without a trace of the resistance that it had had before. It was obedient and friendly.

But Danny hated the dog. He treated it harshly when his father was not around, yelling at it and kicking it for no other reason than that he had perhaps had a bad day at school and felt a measure of catharsis by taking it out on the dog. He hated the dog even more when it reacted only passively to his violence. Most of all, he hated the dog for its obedience to his father—the self-assurance and ease of its submissiveness.

At last, on an instance when his father was not home and when Danny had stretched out his hand to push the dog, the dog finally gave a timid, defensive bite. Although it had not been the worst bite the dog could have inflicted, it had been sufficient to pierce his skin and bruise the flesh around the bite. Danny bandaged himself, but he knew that his father would see—and his father did. When his father inquired about the wound, Danny lied at first. But the wound was obviously a bite, and his father's inquiry was mostly strategic. The dog, meanwhile, stood by his father's side as though nothing out of the ordinary had happened. From its point of view, probably nothing had; it had reacted only as it saw fit, and its reaction had achieved its purpose: Danny had left it alone after that. Danny relented and admitted what had happened, but painted the dog as the aggressor.

Even so, Danny knew that his father understood the full truth about the incident. The dog was loyal. Danny steeled himself for some sort of punishment and for sanctions against his harming the dog any further.

But his father took the dog to the pound.

When his father returned, he had put his hand on Danny's shoulder. His face was hard as iron, but his hand and his gesture communicated an otherwise inexpressible warmth. And that was all; they never spoke of it.

Danny was not sure why this particular story was the one that surfaced in his mind with such intensity during what were sure to be his last moments alive, but it caused him to miss his father terribly. It seemed to him that he had never missed his father so much, not even as a child. He longed for the warm embrace of his thick arms, the rough feel of his father's beard against his own skin, that hand on his shoulder. And because of this desperation, he felt himself believing, despite all of his efforts to the contrary, as Nikki had—that his father was alive, and that he was seeking them now where they no longer were. He could not deny his absolute need, and the need was the belief. The weight of it made his heart sink with an almost physical despair. And he hated himself for this despair; and he hated himself for the absurd hope that he could not control; and he embraced his hatred as the only thing that might buoy up his heart in preparation for his death. He looked to the sides at the others, who hung in what resembled death—the form that he himself would soon assume. Soon, he would be transformed, and then he would starve. He stared into the violent dawn, the sun beginning to rise and scatter the sedate blue of the early hours, and tears came to his eyes. Then he put all thought of his father out of his mind.

He heard a noise in the distance. From his vantage point, he could see the far boundary of the base. To his left was the gate through which he and Nikki had entered, shrouded in trees; directly ahead of him and to his right was the spread of short buildings and minor roads, and beyond them was a tall chain-link fence that barricaded the base that was fortified with barbed wire, strung in lines across the top, which themselves were wrapped in loops of it. The sound had come from beyond the fence.

The morning light was growing stronger and Danny felt his life draining out of him. His body was insupportably heavy. His wrists burned and ached. He struggled even to keep his head upright.

Then the sun finally burst over the horizon at the same time that the horde appeared in the distance. He and Nikki had, in fact, been followed. The light nearly blinded him. The figures were difficult to make out. The dewy air had collected on his cooling forehead, and beads of it rolled into his eyes, distorting the light and blurring his vision of the approaching dead.

The horde had reached the barrier. Those at the front climbed the fence up to the barbed wire. Feeling no pain, they took hold of it with their hands and the jagged metal cut into them. The barbs clung to their flesh, stripping it from them. They climbed up without regard for what was happening to their bodies. They bled dark blood and continued, the wire ripping their muscles, tearing their limbs. The second wave came behind them, pushing those in the first against the wire, driving them farther forward and tearing their bodies apart. This second wave suffered the same. The building clusters of flesh caught in the tangle of wire ripped and spilled slime and vile innards that caught in the chain links as they dropped.

Then a third wave took hold of the fence and drew themselves up. At the top of the fence, they met the indistinguishable mass of the mangled dead that had piled onto the wire, and these met no resistance; they climbed easily over the slippery, shredded bodies and fell freely into the camp, smeared with the blood of their brethren.

The horde spilled over the fence and eventually forced it down altogether, trampling over it, trampling over the wire, trampling over each other.

He watched them, knowing that they would scatter at the sight and smell of their own dead. They would soon part, giving a wide berth to the building and the crosses. They would break ranks and run in a different direction, or many different directions—but they would be driven away. The camp, the last bastion of humanity, would be safe.

The horde approached. He was still alive and sensible for a few moments longer. In the second to last of these, the penultimate moment, the moment before his sight left him, he saw the horde pass under the crosses *undeterred*, united in a common raging chaos—and strike the door with the force of their combined mass, a force that would have broken down a barrier one hundred times as strong, or stronger.

BRAIN GRINDER

When the very ground of the earth had become contaminated, the graveyards yielded up their dead, vomiting them out of the dirt. Kurt and Randall walked through one of these desecrated cemeteries, stepping carefully to avoid falling in the many pits that yawned in black chasms telling of the violence of second birth.

"Grave robbery is against the law," Randall was saying. "What if a man robs his own grave by getting up and walking out of it? What then? Has he still broken the law?"

Randall was the shorter and fairer of the two. Kurt was squarely built, and his dark hair hung over his eyes. Other than their difference in height and color, the two men looked alike.

"Well, his body is his own property," said Kurt. "Can he properly be said to have stolen it?"

"Well, suicide is illegal too. A man's life is his own; yet if he *takes* his own life, it is illegal."

"How can the taking of his own life be properly called taking? It seems to me that if one commits suicide, he *loses* his life. Suicide is not theft at all."

"Would it be considered theft in the sense that you are *taking* yourself away from those who know and love you? In that case, would you be *stealing* yourself away from people who would otherwise have had the chance to interact with you?"

"That implies some sort of right that other people have to you or the experience of you. Don't I have the right to remain silent? Does that include the permanent silencing of my body?"

"No man lives in a vacuum."

"If I am not my own—I mean, if I have no right to myself, whose right am I?"

"Are you?"

"Am I what?"

"Right?"

"Right about what?"

"What you were saying."

"What was I saying?"

"Does it matter?"

"Does what matter?"

"What you were saying?"

"Why wouldn't it matter?"

"Well, it wouldn't matter if you weren't right."

"Was I? Did it?"

"You weren't. But yes."

"Why not, and how come?"

"Because I care about your feelings."

They walked on a little farther. It was getting to be later in the morning, but they couldn't tell exactly what time. A thin layer of white cloud covered the whole sky as though they were in a false world lit with bright light from behind a sheet, but made to resemble the real world, and succeeding to a great extent.

"*A* right," said Kurt.

"What?" said Randall.

"I mean a right belonging to whom am I, not who is."

"Whom am?"

"What?"

"Whom is."

"Whom is what?"

"No, wait—who is."

"Who?"

"Subjective, not objective."

"What is?"

"Everything, I guess."

They walked some more. All around them were the deep gashes where the earth had erupted. Gravestones lay on their backs like old discarded books. The whole of it looked like the set of a play in the midst of being stricken.

"I would never," said Kurt.

"Never what?" said Randall.

"Take my life."

"You can't *take* your own life. You already have it. We talked about this."

"I mean, lose my life. On purpose."

"Oh. Neither would I. Although… if we got separated… then what?"

"Then we would no longer be together."

"Yes, but I mean, what would *happen* after that? What would you *do?*"

"I would… look for you."

"What if you could never find me?"

"What if I could?"

"What if you did, and I was…dead?"

"Would you be?"

"Would I not?"

"Not if I found you alive."

"But if you didn't?"

"Find you?"

"I mean, if I wasn't."

"Alive?"

"Yes. No."

"Then you still might not be *dead*."

"There's the rub. Well, what then?"

"Then you would either be dead, or… not dead."

"Yes, but I mean, what would you *do?*"

"Kill you."

"You mean if I wasn't dead?"

"Weren't. Yes. But not living."

"Right. I would too."

"Would what?"

"Kill you."

"You mean if I wasn't dead?"

"Weren't. Yes. But not living."

"Good."

They were getting hungry. It had been a long time since either of them had seen any of them.

"What if I were alive, but… bitten?" said Randall.

"So, not dead, and not not dead, but going to be?"

"Yes."

"Would I kill you?"

"Yes."

Kurt thought about this for a while.

"Why would I?"

"To keep me from turning."

"Well, then, should I kill you right now? That would keep you from turning."

"But I don't know if I ever will turn."

"Everybody does, sooner or later. You either get bitten and you turn, or you die and you turn."

Randall thought about this for a while. "Unless my brains were blown out. The brain—you have to destroy the brain. It's the only thing that matters."

"Why?"

"Because if the brain is destroyed, you don't turn into one of them. It's a proven fact. And they eat brains, probably to preserve their own brain. Everything a brain needs is in a brain. A brain has what a brain needs."

Kurt nodded, and then said, "Yes, I would kill you."

"I would kill you too." Randall rubbed his hand on his pants, and then held it out: "Let's shake on it."

Kurt extended his hand and took Randall's in his own, sensing the seriousness of the pact.

"We will never let the other one turn," Randall said.

"It's a deal."

"Wait a second," said Randall suddenly. "Where we going?"

"When?"

"Now."

"We're not going anywhere now. We've stopped."

"I mean, in general."

"Death."

"What?"

"In the long run, we're all going to die."

"Well, in the meantime, we need to find food."

"You're right."

They looked down the stretch of the cemetery path on which they were walking and saw that they were nearer the other end than the way they had come in, so they continued walking in the same direction.

"Do laws come from rules or do rules come from laws?" Randall asked.

"What do you mean? Laws *are* rules."

"No, I mean, 'thou shalt not kill'—that's a law. But the idea that you shouldn't kill anyone, that's a rule."

"I see what you mean."

"Well, which came first?"

"Well, somebody probably thought of it before he wrote it down."

"Did he though? Or did he write it down first, and now everyone knows it *because* he wrote it down?"

"Maybe it's the same thing. Maybe a law is a rule if you say so. If enough people say it."

"Yes, I think so. If enough people agree to a law, they probably think that it applies universally."

They walked a little while longer, and Kurt's face grew dark.

"But would that mean then that if everyone agreed murder were not wrong, then murder would be...not wrong?"

"Or maybe just not not right."

"Is something bad only if there is someone there to say so?"

"I suppose."

They continued walking. They were approaching the gate of the cemetery. Kurt felt as though he was having a hard time seeing, even though it was midday. More than once he had almost fallen into an open pit.

The graveyard was at the top of a sloping hill that led to a road cutting through a valley. From the top of the hill, where the gate was, they could see far into the distance. Under the flat, bright gray cloud cover lay vast expanses of derelict farmlands, overgrown now, the boundary lines between the plots of land almost indistinguishable. Everything seemed blurred. There was no sharp light, and there was no shadow. All had blended into a mass of varying but undistinguished shades of gray.

"I wonder what someone would say about us," Kurt said.

"Who?"

"I don't know. Someone who knew us, knew about us, knew what we did, who we were. A historian. What if someone wrote about us in a book?"

Randall sputtered a little. "What does it matter? People who write books are crazy do-nothings. They just sit around and write words. What good are words? Words aren't actually anything, until someone reads them—but who reads them? People who read books are worse than the people who write them. They just sit and sit and stare at symbols on a page that mean essentially nothing— they *think* they mean something, and maybe they do for a while, in their brains, but then it's gone again, and meanwhile time has gone by. What's important is to live in the present, Kurt. Right now is all we have, all we know, all we can count on."

"I think you're right, Randall."

"Besides, who would write about all this? I'd do my best to forget it!"

"Actually, I think it would sell quite well. People love tragedy—as long as it doesn't involve them personally."

They walked through the gate and descended the rolling hill. The tall, overgrown grass whispered against them as they went. Their heavy-duty pants and boots were their work pants and boots, and they had held up. But their shirts were not built for wear; they were stretched and worn thin, and very dirty.

They reached the road at the bottom of the hill, which ran around the rim of it like a wire in a corset.

They walked down the road for some time, side by side, Kurt walking rather slowly but still confidently ahead, and Randall strutting with his hands in his pockets, his hips thrust slightly forward, taking steps that began with an exaggerated and seemingly unnecessary kicking out of the feet.

"What are you thinking about?" Randall asked Kurt finally.

"Nothing," Kurt mumbled.

They walked farther down the road than either expected they would have to before they found an abandoned gas station, the filling area populated by several abandoned cars. Kurt went up to the door of the shop casually, swinging it open and finding nothing inside. It had been so long since they had seen any of them that he had ceased to be very cautious when entering a new place. In fact, he had begun to doubt that they were even still around. It felt as though he and Randall were the last two people on earth.

The shop was empty, and Kurt and Randall went inside. The chalky light came in through the windows enough that they could take stock of what food remained. The store had been well plundered; most of the shelves were empty. All that were left were several identical packages of food—some crunchy corn product that had been rendered unrecognizable from its original form during processing. They tore into these hungrily, eating all of them. While eating them, they thought to themselves to spare some but their hunger got the better of their judgement. In the back of the store was a restroom, filthy from months of use without cleaning. Kurt went in first. He saw his dim reflection in the mirror and was surprised at what he saw. He had seen so little of himself in the past months that he had come to identify himself more with Randall's features, which he saw all the time, than his own. There was still water in the toilet bowl. Randall tried the faucet. It worked, heaving out rhythmic gushes of rusty water. They drank this by the handfuls.

It was getting toward night by the time they decided to leave. They had taken to sleeping in the woods. They were not sure if it was safe or not, but so far, their survival rate suggested that it was.

It was dusk when they left, although the sky had merely dimmed its shade of gray, so that it was difficult to say whether the sun were going down or the clouds merely growing thicker. Because they gauged it only by the darkness of the sky, the passage of time sometimes seemed faster, or slower, than it actually was.

A little way from the convenience store, the road took a sharp left turn and dipped downhill, all the while flanked with tall, dark trees that made it impossible to see down the road farther than a few paces. They were not sure exactly where they were or where they were going, but they had seen signs that had indicated that they should eventually reach a town.

The road led upward again, and then they rounded another bend and emerged on the crest of a hill where the trees cleared and they could look down into another valley, this one containing the promised township. Under the gray sky, the town appeared much like the patchwork of farmlands from whence they had come— blurred, indistinct, gray, and dead.

They descended the steep slope, entering at the edge of the town. Having drawn down to its level and coming out of the trees, they stood on the flat paved ground among the small buildings and walked down the street. They stopped suddenly before they reached the bottom of the road.

In the middle of a dead intersection, stretching across the whole of the road and into an adjoining parking lot, and beyond that even, beyond their ability to see the end of it and the full extent of it, was a pile of human bones. The pile was mountainous, and two of the peaks reached higher than the height of ten men, dwarfing the height of the dark streetlight suspended near it.

After pausing to take in its size, the two men drew nearer to it slowly. At this point, Kurt observed that the pile was darker in shade than the asphalt beneath it. The bones were relatively fresh, still stained with darkening blood and partially studded with bits of black flesh. Not only that, Kurt observed, but there were also chunks of offal piled in with the bones—dark lumps of organs, for the most part—kidneys, livers, bladders, lungs, hearts, intestines, all but the meat. Flies buzzed voraciously about the remains, a chorus of intoxicated ecstasy.

At the first sight of it, Kurt's heart sank and his insides seemed to well up in disgust. He felt an acute revulsion. But then, almost immediately following this reaction, he felt a strange objectivity about it. It appeared to him as only a pile of matter—highly organized, biological matter, swarming with other, more energetic biological matter. He observed it very objectively, and without passion. It quelled his previous reaction, and did not create any new emotion. Its reality, properly and more fully sensed and understood, seemed to make it less real to him.

"What do you make of this?" he said to Randall.

Randall said, "I don't know."

They looked about them. The houses around were as dead as all the others. The unboarded windows were empty and black.

"Maybe this is why we haven't seen anyone," Kurt remarked.

Randall nodded, swallowing. "Could it explain why we haven't seen any of *them* either?"

"How do you mean?"

"Well," said Randall, "perhaps these are not all human remains." He indicated a skull without its top that looked cleanly taken apart, as if it had been cut.

"I see what you mean. But when we kill them, we don't strip the meat off of them."

"True," said Randall, nodding again and putting his hand to his chin. "How many bodies do you think there are altogether in this?"

"I'm terrible at guesses like that," Kurt said. "But I'd say thousands, probably given the fact that there are no muscles. That would make the pile, what, twice as big."

They observed a moment longer.

Finally, Randall said, "What if it's a very large one of them…very large, and very hungry?"

"You mean a giant?"

"Yeah, like a giant… Maybe he rounded up a whole bunch of us, and then sat down and had himself a meal, you know, like we would… suck the meat off of a chicken bone, and toss it away after we were done."

They looked around again. There was no sound; there was no wind. The silence and deadness of it begged Kurt to form his own judgement, as he considered it again as matter and was not repulsed by it.

Instinctively, and at the same moment, they turned away and walked back the way they had come, up the hill they had descended and back into the trees. They walked off of the road and tramped into the dense forest. The sky was beginning to darken heavily now. As they had done before, they found a sequestered patch of ground within the trees that would accommodate their two bodies, and there cleared away the undergrowth until all that remained was the dirt ground. Then they gathered piles of dead branches, mostly cedar, and arranged them into two piles. They laid on these just as the light had grown so dim that it was beginning to be difficult to see. They gathered up dry leaves under their heads, bade each other goodnight, and braced themselves for a night that they knew would bring only fitful, momentary bursts of sleep.

Almost as familiar to them as this routine of clearing ground and gathering the offal of trees was the chorus of sounds that arose during the nighttime hours. From seemingly within the very forest where they rested, and from all the miles beyond within reach of sound, came terrifying cries that echoed rhythmically between hills, through valleys, up inclines, and finally to the glade where the two men lay. The horrible cries were of the nightly orgies performed by the undead—horrible because of their admixture of something very human and familiar with the throaty call of the horde that had come to signify death, destruction, chaos, plague. In those cries, they heard themselves, and they heard something wholly alien, and they were terrified.

The morning light came, bringing the clay-white sky to full illumination gradually, distantly, dispassionately, and the two men awakened. Kurt found that he had drawn himself into the crook of Randall's arm, presumably for warmth—the nights were getting colder and they were without provisions for keeping warm at night. He sat up and breathed in the crisp, dewy air, rubbing his eyes, his senses gradually coming to him. His ears began receiving the forest sounds and the memory of the pile of bones and organs surfaced in his recollection.

Then he realized that the sounds he was hearing were not merely the ambient noises of the forest awaking at dawn, but there was also a continual scuffling noise in the bracken.

He shook Randall, who bolted upright in his bed of leaves. They stood together and looked into the forest surrounding them. It was dense, and they were unable to see far. Looking closely, Kurt detected movement among the branches in the distance. He took hold of Randall's arm and pulled it, turning around and running into the foliage. Randall spun and bolted into the trees, following Kurt.

Kurt dodged shrubs and tree trunks, making his way as fast as he could through the thick growth. He burst out between two tall pine trunks toward the open road, nearly tumbling into the ditch, and then fell out into the paved road, into the open. Then he felt mortified—had he realized his direction, he would have cut to the side and remained in the forest, to try to lose them in it, although it didn't seem to make much difference. They seemed able to track people without the use of any of their senses.

He stood in the middle of the road, chastising himself. Randall burst out of the trees onto the road a moment later. He was more pale than Kurt had ever seen him before. Kurt read the terror on his face to mean that he had been thinking about the pile of bones, that he feared they were being pursued by a giant.

They turned to the tree line from which they had just emerged. At almost the very instant they turned, a number of them burst out of the foliage in a dark cluster, a flurry of ravenous teeth and outstretched hands. The men turned to the opposite bank of trees only to witness the same, a crowd of them hurtling toward them with incomprehensible ferocity and drive.

They met the two on the road, launching into them, their cold fingers brushing their skin. Kurt threw his fists at them, landing a blow against an attacker's face, sending it sprawling, but then another was on his back as his body drew downward with the follow-through, and he fell. Randall was overcome before he had even managed to prime himself for a blow, or some other offensive movement. Two were at his shoulders. They drove their fingers into the muscles of his shoulders, and a third had rushed at him from behind, so that while his arms and shoulders were pulled backward, his head was thrust forward and down, forcing his jaw against his chest and knocking his teeth together. His body twisted around and he too fell to the ground.

Kurt flailed his limbs desperately, but this effort lasted only a moment; before long, they were holding him down by their sheer weight, and had pinned his arms and legs to the road.

Then, he realized the astonishing truth—*they were not eating him.* At this revelation, he ceased his struggling and stared up at them in surprise. They returned his gaze with hollow impassivity. He looked quickly to the side and saw that Russell as well had only been pinned down, although he had suffered more upon impact and was bleeding from the mouth.

With the great strength of their number, they forced Kurt to his feet and held him as though he were a prisoner. They did the same with Randall, who struggled to hold up his head. Once the men were on their feet, the creatures ushered them forward, restraining them only by gripping their wrists. It was at this moment that Kurt finally thought to address them using words—to thank them for sparing his life, as ludicrous as it seemed, or to ask where they were taking them—but the look in their eyes made him think better of it.

So they led the two men on down the road, and before long, they reached the pile of bones and organs that they had encountered the day before. It appeared even larger now. Kurt was not sure if this was due to the difference in the time of day or intensity of light. They led them past this, taking a left at the intersection, and up the town road to the top of another steep ridge.

At the top of the ridge was an old stone church that, judging by the looks of it, had been built around the end of the nineteenth century. It was large—too large for the township in which it resided. Perhaps, thought Kurt, it had been built large in an unfounded optimism that the township would grow more than it actually had or that the membership would increase more than it ever really did. It was derelict, looking to have been abandoned long before even the scourge. Its stone façade had collected mildew that hung in shapes formed and flattened by the pathways of intermittent flows of moisture down the sides.

On the far side of the hill atop which the church stood, the ground was heaped with indeterminate lumps of mass that swarmed with clouds of flies so dense that they resembled smoke. A stench emanated from the church and its grounds that reached them long before they had arrived there. Then they saw others who had been "captured," as Kurt supposed they were, walking along the same road. They were human beings—men and women, like he and Randall, being led by the creatures, some with their wrists held fast, others that had been bound with ties of some sort. They were all being led into the church. It was more activity than Kurt and Randall had seen in a long time. By comparison to their previous weeks of wandering alone down vacant roads, through unpopulated woods, into abandoned settlements and across cemeteries bereft even of the dead, this activity seemed an almost metropolitan bustle.

As they approached the church, the stench grew stronger and more repulsive. Kurt had the impulse to cover his nose, but his hands were still held firmly behind his back.

They were led inside the building, into the church foyer. The room was enclosed under a low ceiling, unlit, and smelling, in addition to the unidentified, overridingly putrid stench, of mildew and decay. The walls were grimy, and the framed pictures and images that had been hung on the wall were discolored and unrecognizable. The floor was littered with scraps of paper that had been trampled and were now completely illegible.

From this room, they were led into the sanctuary, which was an ostentatiously large space that reverberated so fully that it was difficult to distinguish individual sounds in the din that filled it. There was a high balcony that hung over many rows of the pews at the back, accessible by stairs that flanked the rear of the chamber. They led Kurt and Randall up these. By this time, Kurt was beginning to feel acute hunger, and the climb made him feel it all the more, and he became light-headed as they reached the top.

From the top of the balcony, they had a clearer view of the main floor of the sanctuary. The pews had been uprooted from the floor and repurposed into makeshift pens or cells in which people—human beings, like Kurt and Randall—had been herded and confined. They were jammed in so close to one another that they stood one's nose pressed against the other's chin; another's face buried in yet another's slope of the back. There were men, women, and children, and in some cases, children had been herded in together where the only remaining space was in the vertical; they hung on their mother's backs and rested their feet on top of another child's shoulders.

At the front of the church, where the altar had been, there was a cluster of them, hunched around something that they could not see. There came a loud, rending, metallic, almost machine-like sound. There also seemed to be some metal piping that led from the altar to the side of the building, but of this Kurt could not be sure. The front of the church was at a distance that prevented him from making it out in any great detail.

Kurt and Randall were ushered into one of the cells constructed out of pews on the balcony. They stumbled over one another and bumped into a man who was already in the pen. There was still enough room left for them to stand at a distance at which they could look at one another's faces.

The other resident of the cell was a short, middle-aged man with glasses. His head sprouted wisps of hair in a sharp widow's peak that, despite its overgrowth, still did not fully cover his head. The uneven growth of his facial hair told that he wore a moustache in previous life, which had grown out and drooped now like the hands of a clock that no longer told time. He wore thick, heavy glasses that made his eyes look twice as large as they were, although it was clear that he could see nothing. He wore a dirty tweed jacket that, despite having torn at the seams and frayed at the edges, still lent him a bookish, learned look.

"Hello," the man said, in a high-pitched and husky voice. "I'm Dr. Walter Smegma."

Kurt held out his hand first. "Kurt."

Dr. Smegma shook his hand. "Kurt."

Randall gestured likewise. "Randall," he said.

"Randall."

Dr. Smegma smiled at them sunnily, almost as though, it seemed to Kurt, that he was unaware of their current situation— that they had been captured and put into a cell in an abandoned church commandeered by the undead.

"So you're a doctor," Kurt said. "What are you a doctor of?"

"I'm a scientist. Quantum mechanics. Ph.D."

"I see. Did you just get here, too?" Kurt asked him.

"No, I've been here for some time now, some time," said Dr. Smegma. "There was an overflow, and they were only just now able to put me in this cell here. I've been observing them the meanwhile. Fascinating."

"What's fascinating?"

"Why, they are," said the doctor. "At least, from a scientific perspective."

"What's going on here?" asked Randall.

"Processing," answered the scientist.

"What sort of processing?" asked Kurt.

The doctor tilted his head a little to the side, wrinkled his nose, and blinked his eyes. "Food processing."

"What do you mean?"

"Well," said Dr. Smegma, smiling boyishly, "the human brain seems to be their main source of nutrition. In every attack I've witnessed, or that I imagine you've witnessed, the brain is the first thing they consume. Then they will move on to the muscles and consume them, likely for protein. Then they consume the organs last. It seems that these organs provide little or no nutritional value to them, only serving to satiate their appetite, albeit only for a little while. But what they've done here—what they've done is to streamline this whole process. You see, they've rounded us up, and at the front there—" He nearly chuckled as if from giddiness. "At the front, you see, they separate all of the parts. They remove the head from the body, and then they puncture the skull and remove the brain, and send it through a processor that makes a… a brain *sauce*, if you will. Then, you see, they suspend the bodies, headless. They work the arms, holding them up as well, to drain all of the blood from the body. And then they flay the meat from the bones. The remainder is discarded; they eject it from that chute."

He pointed toward the network of pipes at the front of the sanctuary. "It's a very methodical process. It's not very complicated, but it runs like clockwork."

Kurt and Randall stood at the edge of their cell. They stood on their toes and strained their eyes to look to the front of the sanctuary. What the doctor had said was true. The two men watched as, at the front, an automatic saw of some sort bellowed and lowered in pitch as it severed the head of one of the "prisoners." The naked body of the prisoner squirmed momentarily as blood sprayed up out of its neck. Then one of the creatures brought down a large metal hook which it drove through both of the feet of the body. This hook was lifted, hoisting the decapitated body up and hanging it upside down. The same creature lifted the arms, placing the wrists next to the waist of the upside-down figure, and squeezing the soft tissue of the arms. Blood gushed out of the neck into a metal bowl below. Meanwhile, another had taken the head and driven down some sort of piledriver, pulverizing the skull, sending up a wet spurt of blood, and extracted the gray matter, placing it in one of the chutes. After the blood had been drained from the body, the first creature stood next to it and, with the skill of a practiced butcher, separated the meat from the bone, discarding the organs as offal in a bin with the blood. The business was messy. By the end, it was difficult to distinguish which parts of the body were which. Except for scant white patches that revealed bone, it all blended together in a dark, soaked, and spattered hodgepodge, but it was clear that the creatures knew what they were doing. They were behaving automatically, as though programmed.

Kurt stood with his arms crossed, his face twisted into a sneer. But having had it explained to him, he felt a little easier in his skin, and he leaned back comfortably against the cell wall.

"You see?" said Dr. Smegma. "And on the other side of this building is a whole crowd of them, grown fat from the labors of the others in here, no longer exercising from hunting and eating more than they can ever hope to digest."

"I don't know," said Kurt. "This all seems too bizarre. They're not nearly organized enough to—"

"Yes, yes!" exclaimed Dr. Smegma. "That's what we would think, yes. We would think that they were incapable of complex thought, of planning, and organization, such as we have seen here... but we've seen it. You've seen it, gentlemen? We would think that they were only zombies, mindless... but they are clearly much more than that. Much, much more!"

"If they're not zombies, what are they?" asked Kurt.

"I've no idea!" Dr. Smegma exclaimed openly. "But perhaps we've been wrong about them all this time."

"But we've never seen—" Kurt began. Then he checked himself. He cupped his chin in his hand and gazed at the floor. The floor was filthy, and the concrete was cracked. "How could this happen?"

"How does *anything* happen?" said Dr. Smegma. "Biology! It must have been in their programming to become self-organizing. It was inevitable—only a matter of time. From chaos comes order."

Kurt's senses had acclimated to the vile stench that permeated the air, but a new wave of nausea hit him.

"Fascinating," Dr. Smegma repeated.

Meanwhile, Randall's face had grown white and moisture collected on it. Although the sanctuary was hot and the air humid, Randall was sweating also in a rage. "It's inhuman," he said at last.

"Well, of course," Dr. Smegma said. "They are not human."

"I mean, it's cruel and disgusting," said Randall, his voice quavering. "It's...abominable. How can you simply say it's 'fascinating'?"

"Well, perhaps my scientist's training has taught me to be *too* objective," he said. "But look at the precision with which they operate. And furthermore, I have not witnessed any verbal communication between them. How do they know which stations to take? How does the one know what the other is doing? Is it, perhaps, like the activity of bees, where different castes are designed to perform certain functions—drones, workers, and so forth? Or rather, as I am more inclined to suspect given their connection to us as humans, do they communicate through some higher sense? Telepathy, perhaps?"

"Who the fuck cares?" blurted Kurt.

"Well, I admit my concerns are likely motivated by my academic predilections, but of course, you may care if you care for your own survival. I myself began to seek to understand the zombie (if he is indeed a zombie) and how he operates in order to learn best how to avoid or defeat him. You may, however, discover that he represents a higher order of life-form than yourself, and that your own survival is a concern only relative yourself, unimportant in the face of the overall thrust of…evolution."

"So you're saying," said Kurt with an intentional note of insolence and disgust, "is that they are the next step in evolutionary progress? That they're better than us?"

"Ah, no, not even that—" exclaimed Dr. Smegma, holding up a finger. "Even 'progress' and 'better' are relative terms. Those words are loaded with what we have already decided must be progressive, or superior, an appeal to some sort of system of our own. But you see, what is repulsive to us has no bearing in the long run. There is only what survives and what does not, and only by this advancement is a thing justified. Persistence is its own justification. Had we been able to weather this out, defeated the zombie—only *then* would we have been justified in judging ourselves superior to the zombie. But here we sit, we three, in this little cell, awaiting our decapitation and dismemberment—what grounds do we have to say that we are 'better,' or even that we are 'worse' than they? No, I will not debate with you and contend that they are 'better' while you say that they are 'worse.' I merely point to the fact that they have beaten us. That is all. 'Better' and 'worse' are ideas that we invent—and when we are swept away, they will matter no longer."

Randall was visibly disturbed. His face had contorted and there were tears in his eyes. Kurt was still going over what Dr. Smegma had said, when Randall flared up.

"We can clearly see what is better and what is worse—what is good and what is bad! How can anyone look at *that* and say that it is neither?"

"I can."

"But, what about…*humanity?*"

144

"What of it? Humanity is biology. Consider the Sphex wasp. A Sphex is a carnivorous insect that paralyzes its prey to take it to its nest. But before it brings its prey into its nest, it inspects the nest first to make sure that it is fit for the prey. Then it emerges, relocates the prey, and drags it into the nest. *But*—if the prey is moved, by say, an experimenter, and the Sphex emerges from the nest after inspection to find the prey missing, it relocates the moved prey, drags it to the nest, but then *re-inspects* the nest. Its programming has been reset. It will continue to do this as long as the experimenter moves the prey.

"Gentlemen, it is no different with us—we are operating according to our own programming which, admittedly, is much more complex, but nonetheless similar. And as you see, the zombie is operating according to his own programming, more complex than our own. It therefore seems strange to us, and perhaps we even see fit to pass a moral judgment on it. But I ask you, is it not merely a higher form of order? And in this case, is it not to be embraced?"

Randall was nearly shaking with rage. "Can a zombie *love?*" he uttered vehemently. He moved closer to Kurt, as though to stand next to him offered some sort of solidarity in this conflict.

Dr. Smegma seemed less interested. "Love is a biological impulse. If you mean the attachment to a romantic mate, a partner, then I have no idea. You know that they copulate. No doubt you have heard it, as I have. In either case, it does not much matter. Even if 'love' were a 'thing' that we possessed and the zombie did not, that is not yet grounds on which to dismiss the zombie as inferior."

Kurt was growing more uncomfortable and found that he could identify with neither Randall nor Dr. Smegma. He was repulsed by both of them.

"From chaos comes order," repeated the doctor, "and from lower orders come higher orders. You may resist it if you choose. *I* choose, rather, to embrace the inevitable."

Randall locked his arms together across his chest and turned abruptly in a refusal to engage any further. Dr. Smegma turned, smiling, to Kurt.

"And what was it that you used to do?" he asked conversationally.

"We were gravediggers," said Kurt.

Dr. Smegma made a noise like "ah," and turned to watch the activity below.

Kurt directed his gaze once more to the floor and saw that, among the filth that littered the ground was a metallic object that reflected the light, sparkling. He bent down, brushed aside the clods of dust and human waste in which it was embedded, and picked it up. It was a child's music box—without electricity, probably the only object that could reproduce music for a child. He turned the crank, and almost in the instant that it plunked out its tune, the words arose in his memory:

London bridge is falling down
Falling down, falling down...

He thought about the child who had likely owned this music box—a child who had had a greater fraction of its life consumed by dread of the zombie. Had the child listened to this tune to remember its home, its previous life? Had it listened to remember a lost loved one, perhaps even its mother? Did it recall these memories to console itself from the constancy of death, the knowledge of its own imminent annihilation? Kurt felt as though a thread that he had been working to unravel had just doubled back on itself and become hopelessly tangled forever.

There was a commotion at the boundary of their cell, and one of the planks was pulled away. Their time had come. A zombie pulled first at Dr. Smegma who, still smirking, followed with what seemed almost to be excitement. Randall flailed as they came for him, but they soon subdued him and brought him out of the cell behind the doctor. Finally, they came for Kurt who submitted more out of apathy and weariness than the active cooperation of the scientist, and dropped the music box to the floor.

They descended the stairs, emerging onto the main level of the sanctuary. They walked forward amidst the awful din between the rows of wooden enclosures, and Kurt once again became aware of the horrible stench as it grew stronger at his approach. He looked at the pens as they passed, but the boards were too high to make out who, if anyone, was inside.

They brought Dr. Smegma up to the front of the church, where the altar used to be, where the machinery for human processing was. They stripped his clothes off with great efficiency, and he willingly obliged, helping them with their efforts. He removed his glasses, revealing how miniscule his eyes really were, blinking them in blindness at his surroundings. They laid him down, naked, in the machine, and the blade, powered mysteriously by something other than electricity—Kurt saw no wires or sources of power—began its awful whirr.

Suddenly, the two zombies who were attending Randall howled loudly, the noise blending with the noise of the saw. The saw ceased, and those operating the machinery bellowed and clambered down from the platform.

All throughout the sanctuary, the zombies broke from their stations and descended on the cells, tearing down the makeshift wooden structures, splintering and breaking the wood and throwing it aside. The cells were still packed as full as they had been when Kurt and Randall had arrived. The zombies attacked the people still inside, pulling them from the confines of the cell, tearing at them with their fingers and their teeth, ripping the flesh from their bones, cracking their skulls on the cement floor, devouring the brains, devouring the muscles, drinking down the fluids, discarding nothing, bathing the sanctuary with sprays and gushes of blood in a melee of carnage.

In the confusion, Kurt managed to find Randall, and pulled him by the arm as several attacked from behind, nearly knocking him down. He lifted Randall to his feet and they dove into the thick mass of ravenous zombies.

As they made their way through, Kurt caught a glimpse of Dr. Smegma at the front of the church, where the altar used to be. The operation had stopped with Dr. Smegma's head partly severed. His naked body lay limp. His expression was neutral, the smirk finally gone, and blood had erupted from his eyes as though he had seen something for the first time and wept bitterly at it with tears of blood. The inert machinery was a mere jumble of metal to no purpose. Kurt doubted that he had seen what he had earlier, and discarded it from his memory and his mind, although he was newly filled with horror. The illusion of order had vanished, and the sense of relief that he had felt when he was in the cell was gone.

Pulling Randall behind him, Kurt pushed his way through the horde. Some were locked in bloodthirsty frenzy, blind to all but that on which they were already feasting. Others stalked the sanctuary in zeal, running and bounding after any moving person that caught their attention. A quick hand snatched at Kurt; he turned, throwing a punch, making contact with something—he couldn't see what. He drew back his fist, now covered in blood and filth. Another swiped at him from behind; he lurched backward onto it, driving it down to the ground. He thrust his elbow behind him, connecting painfully with its ribs and snapping them. Two leapt over him while he was down; he thrust both his hands in the air in an instinctive motion of defense. His left hand struck the zombie on the chin, and the fingers of his right hand thrust deep into the other zombie's mouth. The zombie bit down, cleaving through his bones with a crunch and severing his fingers. In a shock of pain, he lurched forward, throwing the offending zombie off. He looked to his right and saw that Randall had been brought to the ground and that two were pulling at his leg mercilessly and with such a force that they had bent the foot out of joint. Kurt dove forward and took hold of him by the torso. He pulled hard, as hard as he felt that he could. The others pulled also, and with a crack, the ankle joint broke and the skin tore and the foot separated from Randall's body. Randall screamed in pain. Kurt, with his arms wrapped around Randall's torso, fell with him to the floor. Then he hooked his elbow under Randall's other arm, and pulled him free.

There was an exit to the side of the sanctuary that, Kurt assumed, led out of the church entirely. When they reached it, he kicked the door open and discovered that he was right—the door opened to the blinding, formless, white sky, filling the entire doorway. They fell out of the door into the blank emptiness.

Past the door was a small courtyard, and then a rolling hill populated by the bloated zombies that had been feeding on all who had been herded into the church until now. They all sat together on the ridge, their bodies beside and on top of one another, as though they had stopped moving long ago but continued growing long after they had run out of space to grow. Some had grown over while others had grown under. Kurt and Randall rolled down the hill of fat zombies whose heads rolled around in their necks, searching the air with their tongues like barnacles. Some of the bodies were so plump that their skin burst at impact, their bodies exploding wetly like overripe fruit. Kurt and Randall tumbled down to the bottom where the zombies ceased to have any sort of definition from one to the other—they were no longer individuals, but the hill became merely a sea of fleshy mouths and tongues. The zombies had nearly liquefied, bearing only featureless mouths that opened up passively in an amorphous, gelatinous mass.

Kurt's vision began to fail, and it was with great difficulty that he managed to drag Randall away from the globby slime onto an empty patch of pavement, as though he had just emerged from a womb. They were covered with blood, filth, and pulpy jelly from head to foot. On his hands and knees, Kurt sputtered and wiped it away, while Randall lay on the ground gasping for breath as his blood stained the asphalt. For how serious the injury was, it did not seem to be causing a great loss of blood. Kurt lifted his head and sat on the ground beside Randall and looked back up the hill.

They were looking at the back of the church now, up the hill of fat zombies. Seen from this side, it looked entirely different. It seemed small and insignificant from the ground. Their experience inside seemed to Kurt to be a mere dream, something of little or no consequence. They were back on the ground, and things were as they had always been, and would always continue to be. They had escaped, and escaped alive, although for how much longer neither of them could say.

Kurt tore his shirt from his body and tied it around Randall's lower leg as a tourniquet. Randall winced in pain. The bleeding seemed to slow, but did not stop. Kurt pulled the knot of his shirt tighter and Randall cried out, but the bleeding seemed to continue at the same rate.

"I don't know," said Kurt. "I don't know what I can do."

Randall rolled on his back and sputtered a laugh. "I always had two left feet," he said.

"I would *never* have left you," said Kurt.

Kurt put his arm around Randall again and lifted him up, placing him unsteadily on his one good foot.

He led him like this away from the church toward the road that led out of the town in the opposite direction from which they had entered it. He wasn't sure where it would take them, but the open road seemed like a safer bet than going back to either the woods or into the town. It led away straight; they could see down the road a considerable distance.

As they went down the road, they did not talk. Randall grunted as he strained to remain upright and maintain his balance. Kurt strained too under Randall's unsteady weight. Randall's head hung low and Kurt leaned in close to him. From a distance, they would have looked like an intimate couple speaking to each other softly. The white sky hung over them like a screen.

Kurt looked back over his shoulder. They had progressed a good distance, but had not gone as far as he would have liked. He could still see the church on the hill, its dinginess the only thing that separated it from the chalky sky. It was a good landmark, Kurt thought. Once they were out of sight of it, then he would feel safe to rest.

The road was flanked on both sides with old-style houses that stood on large pieces of property. The grass lawns were overgrown. A tree had fallen on one, and the roof had caved in. They passed a road sign that said, WATER OVER ROADWAY. But it had not rained for several days, and the road was dry.

The road had been straight and easy, but before long, they passed a sign that read LIMITED SIGHT DISTANCE, and it took a sharp and sudden curve down a hill along the edge of a steep drop, the severity of which was masked by the dense foliage that grew on it. The guardrail had been bent and twisted from the edge, likely from an accident long ago where someone had barreled through it and driven over the edge. As they were walking, it was easy to maneuver the curve that, for a car, would have been treacherous.

The trees became thicker down the curve, blocking out the sky. The air grew colder. A clammy chill descended on Kurt, and he became aware that he was gradually growing nauseous. He felt a burning sting on his shoulder. Thinking it to be muscle pain, he reached up his free hand to massage it. His fingers found an open wound, sticky with warm blood. Then he remembered that he had been bitten at the church. He coughed and shook his head. He put the thought out of his mind. They were out of sight of the church. The next priority was finding some sort of shelter. When they came to something that would suffice, he thought, then he would stop and rest and deal with the wound.

At the bottom of the incline, Randall stumbled on his foot and rolled his ankle. His weight shifted suddenly, and Kurt did not have time to adjust his footing before he lost hold of him. Randall fell to the side of the road where the guardrail had been uprooted and fell through the gap into the foliage, and then he rolled away down the hill. Kurt had lost his balance as well and fell into the guardrail at the point where it had been bent. The metal had been folded into a sharp angle like the point of a wedge; it dug into Kurt's side like a knife as he fell on it. His body continued to fall, and he tumbled into the bracken lining the edge of the road after Randall. He rolled down the hill through the brush, past an abandoned car—likely the one that had crashed through the guardrail long ago. He threw his hands out in front of him in an effort to slow his descent, but his hands found nothing to hold on to. He had tucked his legs in underneath him and his exposed knees struck a heavy limb that had fallen. His kneecaps cracked against it and pain shot through the length of his legs.

Not far down, the ground leveled and there was a clear patch of stumps overgrown with brush. Kurt landed on his ribs against the corner of a stump crowned with a snarl of blackberry vine. His ribs cracked against the stump and the thorns cut his skin. His legs ached with pain. He knew his legs were useless.

Randall was not far from him, his face cut and smeared with blood, twigs and shoots sprouting from his hair like the remnants of a crown of weeds. He saw Kurt's fall and observed his unnaturally straight legs, his side gaping and bloody, and he began to weep.

Kurt was dazed from the fall, but after a moment, his senses returned to him somewhat. He noted the blackberries, how they were ripening already. Nature was a machine, he thought, and it was a perfect machine. It never broke; it always continued to operate. Why had humanity never been able to build a machine like that?

He looked up at Randall, blurred in his hazy vision. He had sustained a blow to the head on his way down, and he attempted to lift his arm to touch it, but his arm did not respond. He looked down at it. It was grey, colorless—it was broken, and it had already begun to decay.

He looked back up at Randall's blood- and tear-stained face and a mutual glance confirmed between them what they both knew: this was it. And Randall began to weep more deeply, taking in shallow gasps of breath and blurting out short sobs.

"I'm turning…" said Kurt, weakly. As he spoke, sharp pain stung deep in his side; the metal must have pierced him deeper than he had thought.

Randall blinked his eyes and brought his weeping under control and looked around for a something that might serve as a weapon, but gave up quickly.

"I'm too far away," he said. "I don't have anything…"

"Fuck," said Kurt, rolling his head back and closing his bloody eyes.

They fell into silence, sitting in the clearing, neither able to move. All around them the forest was quiet, and the white sky hovered above them with silent warmth.

"Kurt," said Randall.

Kurt rolled his head down again and opened his eyes. "Yeah."

"There's something I—that I have to tell you. That I always wanted to tell you before you—before we—" His throat caught and he emitted another heavy sob.

"What is it?" said Kurt.

"I—I—" Randall struggled, and then shivered violently with a sudden chill. He was losing blood. He took in a deep, stuttering breath and, with his voice quavering so much that it nearly impeded his intelligibility:

"I love you."

Kurt looked at him slowly out of one eye. He took in a breath and said, "I… I love you too, man."

Randall slurped in a breath wet with blood and phlegm and said, "No, Kurt, I—I *love* you."

Kurt looked at him again out of one eye, this time saying nothing.

"I've loved you since we met…" he said. "Since your first day digging graves…"

Kurt winced. "So was that… was our friendship…? You mean, the whole time…?"

"Yes, but… our friendship was real too…"

Kurt was in so much pain that he could not determine if the overwhelming sense of disgust that struck him was the result of Randall's confession or the cumulative effect of his injuries. He felt as though an inconceivable distance had grown between them, some interminable gulf opened up that dwarfed their physical distance from each other lying immobile in the glade.

"I don't…" said Kurt, cut off by another stab of pain.

"I love to be with you," said Randall, babbling more freely. "All I ever wanted was to spend forever by your side. We trust each other… I always knew that we were perfect companions. I was afraid that you wouldn't understand. I just wanted to be with you in every way. I wanted us to be close. I wanted to be a shoulder for you to lean your head on, to nestle into…"

A wave of nausea washed over Kurt. He found it difficult to follow Randall's words. They meant nothing to him. And then he thought again of the church, of the pile of corpulent zombies, the morbidity and the stench, the living rot.

The sky grew brighter, and for a moment, the clouds threatened to dissipate, hinting at the presence of the sun, a definite position of the source of the light by which they saw. On the ground, the world glowed brighter, shadows threatened to form—the pale world suggested more color, more definition, starker contrast of brightness and darkness. And the forest ceased to be merely mechanical; it took on a character of otherness, of ghostliness. The forest was haunted—the forest itself haunted him. Everything was alive in the fullest sense of the word. The trees, the bracken—all was imbued with an otherworldly transcendence. But this it did for only a moment, and then the clouds thickened again and the world was cloaked in white and gray. There were no shadows, and there was no sun.

For a moment, Kurt thought that he saw something on the edge of his vision, like a shadow, or another, similar darkness. Then he was struck with an overwhelming sense of fatigue, of sleepiness.

Nausea overwhelmed him. He lost all sense. And then he was dead.

Randall heaved a sigh as though he would begin weeping uncontrollably again, but he was spent and the sigh died in him.

Then Kurt woke up. His eyes clicked open revealing irises clouded over with grey, insensate nothingness governing a lack of vision.

The knees cracked and the body lifted itself up with a locomotion that seemed external to its being and it stood up on its contorted legs. It moved toward Randall, devoid of emotion, looking toward him but not at him, alive but not living, and terribly ravenous. Randall's eyes had fallen to the forest floor, and they did not rise. The creature that was Kurt bowed its head over him, gently rested its head on the nape of his neck, caressing his shoulder with the hair of its head. It brushed its lips against his skin. Randall shivered. It exhaled lightly, and then it sank its teeth into his skin.

THE END

CHECK OUT OTHER GREAT ZOMBIE NOVELS

DEAD ASCENT
by Jason McPhearson

The dead have risen and they are hungry...

Grizzled war veteran turned game warden, Brayden James and a small group of survivors, fight their way through the rugged wilderness of southern Appalachia to an isolated cabin in the hope of finding sanctuary. Every terrifying step they make they are stalked by a growing mass of staggering corpses, and a raging forest fire, set by the government in hopes of containing the virus.

As all logical routes off the mountain are cut off from them, they seek the higher ground, but they soon realize there is little hope of escape when the dead walk and the world burns.

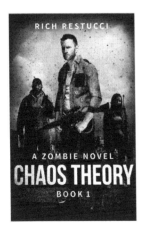

CHAOS THEORY
by Rich Restucci

The world has fallen to a relentless enemy beyond reason or mercy. With no remorse they rend the planet with tooth and nail.

One man stands against the scourge of death that consumes all.

Teamed with a genius survivalist and a teenage girl, he must flee the teeming dead, the evils of humans left unchecked, and those that would seek to use him. His best weapon to stave off the horrors of this new world? His wit.

CHECK OUT OTHER GREAT ZOMBIE NOVELS

RUN
by Rich Restucci

The dead have risen, and they are hungry.

Slow and plodding, they are Legion. The undead hunt the living. Stop and they will catch you. Hide and they will find you. If you have a heartbeat you do the only thing you can: You run.

Survivors escape to an island stronghold: A cop and his daughter, a computer nerd, a garbage man with a piece of rebar, and an escapee from a mental hospital with a life-saving secret. After reaching Alcatraz, the ever expanding group of survivors realize that the infected are not the only threat.

Caught between the viciousness of the undead, and the heartlessness of the living, what choice is there? Run.

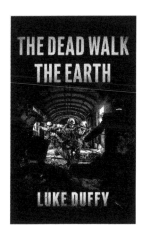

THE DEAD WALK THE EARTH
by Luke Duffy

As the flames of war threaten to engulf the globe, a new threat emerges.

A 'deadly flu', the like of which no one has ever seen or imagined, relentlessly spreads, gripping the world by the throat and slowly squeezing the life from humanity.

Eight soldiers, accustomed to operating below the radar, carrying out the dirty work of a modern democracy, become trapped within the carnage of a new and terrifying world.

Deniable and completely expendable. That is how their government considers them, and as the dead begin to walk, Stan and his men must fight to survive.

CHECK OUT OTHER GREAT
ZOMBIE NOVELS

900 MILES
by S. Johnathan Davis

John is a killer, but that wasn't his day job before the Apocalypse.

In a harrowing 900 mile race against time to get to his wife just as the dead begin to rise, John, a business man trapped in New York, soon learns that the zombies are the least of his worries, as he sees first-hand the horror of what man is capable of with no rules, no consequences and death at every turn.

Teaming up with an ex-army pilot named Kyle, they escape New York only to stumble across a man who says that he has the key to a rumored underground stronghold called Avalon..... Will they find safety? Will they make it to Johns wife before it's too late?

Get ready to follow John and Kyle in this fast paced thriller that mixes zombie horror with gladiator style arena action!

WHITE FLAG OF THE DEAD
by Joseph Talluto

Millions died when the Enillo Virus swept the earth. Millions more were lost when the victims of the plague refused to stay dead, instead rising to slaughter and feed on those left alive. For survivors like John Talon and his son Jake, they are faced with a choice: Do they submit to the dead, raising the white flag of surrender? Or do they find the will to fight, to try and hang on to the last shreds or humanity?

CHECK OUT OTHER GREAT ZOMBIE NOVELS

Z BURBIA
by Jake Bible

Whispering Pines is a classic, quiet, private American subdivision on the edge of Asheville, NC, set in the pristine Blue Ridge Mountains. Which is good since the zombie apocalypse has come to Western North Carolina and really put suburban living to the test!

Surrounded by a sea of the undead, the residents of Whispering Pines have adapted their bucolic life of block parties to scavenging parties, common area groundskeeping to immediate area warfare, neighborhood beautification to neighborhood fortification.

But, even in the best of times, suburban living has its ups and downs what with nosy neighbors, a strict Home Owners' Association, and a property management company that believes the words "strict interpretation" are holy words when applied to the HOA covenants. Now with the zombie apocalypse upon them even those innocuous, daily irritations quickly become dramatic struggles for personal identity, family security, and straight up survival.

ZOMBIE RULES
by David Achord

Zach Gunderson's life sucked and then the zombie apocalypse began.

Rick, an aging Vietnam veteran, alcoholic, and prepper, convinces Zach that the apocalypse is on the horizon. The two of them take refuge at a remote farm. As the zombie plague rages, they face a terrifying fight for survival.

They soon learn however that the walking dead are not the only monsters.

Made in the USA
Lexington, KY
23 September 2017